MY MONTICELLO

MY MONTICELLO

FICTION

JOCELYN NICOLE JOHNSON

THORNDIKE PRESS
A part of Gale, a Cengage Company

Copyright © 2021 by Jocelyn Nicole Johnson.
"Control Negro" originally appeared in *Guernica* in 2017; "Virginia Is Not Your Home" originally appeared in *Phoebe Journal* in 2020; "The King of Xandria" originally appeared in *Prime Number* in 2016.
Thorndike Press, a part of Gale, a Cengage Company.

LIBRARY OF CONGRESS CIP DATA ON FILE.
CATALOGUING IN PUBLICATION FOR THIS BOOK
IS AVAILABLE FROM THE LIBRARY OF CONGRESS.

ISBN-13: 978-1-4328-9412-2 (hardcover alk. paper)

Published in 2022 by arrangement with Henry Holt and Company

Printed in Mexico
Print Number: 01   Print Year: 2022

For my parents,
who had me in Virginia
and made it home.

CONTENTS

CONTROL NEGRO

By the time you read this, you may have figured it out. Perhaps your mother told you, though she was only privy to my timeworn thesis — never to my aim or full intention. Still, maybe the truth of it breached your insides:

That I am your father, that you are *my* son.

In these typewritten pages I mean to make manifest the truth, the whole. But please do not mistake this letter for some manner of veiled confession. I cannot afford to be sorry, not for any of it. I hope you'll come to understand, it was all for a grander good.

You see, I needed a Control Negro, grotesque as that may sound —

You should know I was there on the day you were born, a reflection behind the nursery glass. I laid eyes on you while your mother rested, along with her husband — that man you must have accepted, at least for a time, as your father. You seemed to see me too, my blurred silhouette. Your birth (natural, vaginal) took place at the university's teaching hospital. I noted your weight (7 lb., 7 oz.), your color (dark and florid), your temperament (outwardly placid) — like mine.

I assisted with payment for your daycare as well, when you were so small, still in those plush white Pampers. The facility sat at the edge of campus. So graduate students, like your mother, could enroll their young children while they worked or studied. And faculty, like me, could take guided tours and observe through mirrored one-way glass. I took mental notes on the room of children, a rainbow of faces, but my eyes hung on you: your mahogany skin and dark, keen eyes. Your fat, curled fingers grasping at blocks, trying to build something sturdy and true. I grew skilled at enduring the feeling you inspired, a seeping pride that filled my chest, then spilled into a painful ache.

Remember your season of Little League games, the ones at Washington Park, just down from the bus stop? I could always spot you, especially at a distance. You'd be standing at the plate, arms angled, aiming for the bright white ball, determined to hit it past every boundary we could see.

What I mean to say is that all this time I've watched you, or else had others watch in my stead. My TA did a practicum with your sixth-grade civics teacher. One of my graduate students tutored you in middle school at my suggestion that he "give something back." He shared anecdotes of your progress, never suspecting that you were mine. Your sophomore year, I hired a college student, a young man of legal age but slight enough to pass for seventeen. You knew him as David from the neighboring county. Under my direction he befriended you, prodded you toward swimming (and away from the fraught cliché of basketball). He ferried me printouts of your correspondence, revealing your vernacular speech, the slant of your smile in cell phone pictures. Hearing this now, you might feel manipulated, violated even. But I am almost certain that my determination to shape and groom, my attempts and failures to protect, aren't terribly different from those of any other parent.

Everyone has an origin story and this is yours: You began as a thought fully formed and sprung from my head. No, you were more like a determined line of questions marching altogether toward a momentous thrashing. It was 1985, years before you

11

were born, and I'd just come to work here on this campus. Mother died at the start of fall semester, her body inundated with cancer, undiagnosed until she had passed. Numb, I traveled south to bury her, missing the initiation of my own first classes, returning as promptly as I could. I was only away for a week and a day, but a cold snap had scattered leaves onto the great lawn. My first afternoon back, I walked over to my office and was straightening the objects on my desk, my shirtsleeves rolled up, my back to the door. A man walked in and he startled when I turned to face him, so I startled too. He was — I learned a few minutes later — a senior colleague from my own department: history. He'd been away on sabbatical and had come to my office to welcome me. "Sorry," he said. "I'm looking for a Professor Adams. Do you know where I can find him, buddy?" I realized what was happening a moment before he did, and forced myself to laugh, to try to put him at ease, though I fear my laughter came out as a strangled sound. You see, he'd mistaken me for one of the evening janitors.

But then, the next week, I stood before all of my bright young students. For the first time in a long time, I felt, if not settled, then at least situated. Soon afterward, in a morning seminar, I remember feeling hopeful as I collected an early set of in-class writings, our topic: nineteenth-century thinkers. I discovered a hand-drawn cartoon among the shuffle, no name in the corner, passed in on purpose or by accident — it was hard to tell which. It was nothing really, just a single frame of itchy graphite titled "Irony." Within its borders, a history professor leaned over a lectern, looking quite like me — same jacket and bowtie — except with something primitive about his face. A thought bubble hovered over the room of students: "Darwin Taught to Men by an Ape."

It's nothing, I told myself as I walked back to my apartment that evening, though, in truth, I felt — tired. What does it matter, I remember thinking. What does it matter how much I achieve, or how clearly I speak, or how carefully I conduct myself, if the brutal misjudgments remain regardless? What if, even here, they cannot bring themselves to see me, and instead see something oblique reflected where I thought I stood? Mother used to tell me, Work hard, Cornelius. Work twice as hard and you can have something. But there I was, a grown man, wondering what it was I could have, and what would forever be withheld.

What I needed, it occurred to me then, was to watch another man's life unfold: a Black boy not unlike me, but better than me — an African American who was otherwise equivalent to those broods of average American Caucasian males who scudded through my classrooms. ACMs, I came to call them, and I wondered how they would measure up with this flawless young man as a watermark. No, it wasn't them exactly — I wanted to test my own beloved country: Given the right conditions, could America extend her promise of Life and Liberty to me too, to someone like me? What I needed was a control, a Control Negro. And given what I teach, it wasn't lost on me, the agitation of those two words linked together, that archaic descriptor clanking off the end like a rusted shackle.

Those words struck in me and, from them, you grew.

That was the start of my true research, a secret second job hidden inside of the rigors of my first one. Evenings and weekends I searched library stacks, scoured journals and published studies. I focused on contemporary ACMs, looking for patterns, for cause and effect. An ACM's access to adequate childhood nutrition up against disciplinary referrals resulting in primary

14

school suspensions. An ACM's expected time with his father (watching the game, I imagined, practicing catch), versus police reports of petty vandalism, of said balls careening through a neighbor's window. I was determined to measure the relationship of support, to action, to *re*-action, to autonomy in these young men. At some point it occurred to me to work backward. I gathered a more intimate sample: twenty-five case files borrowed from the university's records, culled from a larger random pool. Each of these ACMs came from families of high middle income, had an average or slightly above average IQ, had a face that approached symmetry as determined by his student ID photo. In my pursuit to better understand them, I called suburban high schools, interviewed teachers, coaches, parents even, always over the phone — I was less than forthright, I concede. My ACMs were all "good" promising young men, but they were flawed too, if you scratched the surface. My dredging uncovered attention deficit disorder, depression, vandalism, drug and alcohol abuse. In several cases, I found evidence of more serious transgressions: assault and battery; accusations of sexual misconduct. Not one of these young men was perfect, yet each held promise, and this promise, on balance, was enough to protect them and to buoy their young lives into the future. Five years of my life spent marveling at the resiliency of theirs.

Now all I had to do was monitor a boy who enjoyed, on average, the same lifted circumstances that my ACMs had experienced. Prenatal care and regular visits to the dentist. An educated mother and father (or father figure). Well-funded schools and a residence situated in a "good," safe neighborhood. For his part, this young man would have to keep his grades up, have clear diction, wear his pants at an average perch at his waist. He would have to present a moderate temperament, maybe twice as moderate — just to be safe — as those bright boys he'd be buffed so hard to mirror.

What I aimed to do was to painstakingly mark the route of this Black child too, one who I could *prove* was so strikingly decent and true that America could not find fault in him unless we as a nation had projected it there.

About this time, I met your mother.

What can I say — she was, in her own way, a force of nature, and the sole woman of color in the graduate program in environmental studies that year. I spotted her one rainy afternoon in a dimly lit classroom. The door half open, she stood at the lectern rehearsing, her PowerPoint blinking furiously behind her, projecting light and shadow on her face. Slide after slide of washed-out shores and water rising. She looked up at me but did not lose her place. It would be only one more year before you were born.

Our first night together, your mother informed me she was married — she intended to *remain* married — which came as a relief. Those early years of struggle had made me a solitary sort of man. Nonetheless we continued to see each other, sporadically, into the spring. She wanted a child, I knew, and although her husband was likely the source of her childlessness, to protect his pride she alone bore the blame between them. That winter when I found out you were growing inside her, part mine and a boy, we both agreed. I would contribute financially and keep silent about my paternity. She would keep you nearby and take my requests about you to heart. She knew about my ACMs, but never that I needed a boy to balance them. Right then and there, I realized who you would be.

There are many studies now about the

17

cost of race in this great nation. Most convincing is the work from other departments: sociology, cultural anthropology. Researchers send out identical résumés or home loan applications, half of which are headed with "ethnic-sounding" names. They instruct Black and white individuals to watch other Black and white individuals receive a painful-looking shot. The needle digs into muscle and the researchers mark how much sweat leaks from pores of the watchers. They measure who gets the job, the loan, who gets the lion's share of salted, dank empathy. They mark which colored human-shaped targets get shot by police, in study after study, no matter how innocuous the silhouetted objects they cradle. All these studies, I concede, are good, great work, but I wonder, is there something flawed in them that makes the findings too easy to dismiss?

My research, by contrast, has been more personal — challenging me, at times, to reexamine my history. How different my life has been from the lives of my ACMs, and from your life. You grew up on that tree-lined cul-de-sac, while I was born in the back room of a two-room house, in the sand hills of South Carolina. I was a dark-skinned bookish child — we both are only sons. My

18

own mother didn't have much money, but no one had much. Certainly not any of the colored folks we knew, the only point of comparison one dared in those days. Most of my schoolmates had fathers, though, and mine had gone north, to Chicago, for work, and not come back. He was essentially a stranger. Even so, growing up, I felt his abandonment acutely, like hunger. I filled that hunger with reading.

Like you, I played baseball, if briefly. The summer I turned ten I joined the Negro Youth League. I went for the promised uniforms, which turned out to be sweat-stained cast-offs salvaged from a white church's collection. Even so, thick patches had been sewn onto the chests, and underneath mine, my heart felt sanctioned. Our very first practice, I managed a decent hit, a satisfying thwack like an ax cleaving wood. Afterward, I should have walked back with the others, but instead I set off on my own, replaying my minuscule victory in my head until it felt epic and novel-worthy. I wandered down behind White Knoll, crossing Main, still dreaming. I didn't realize where I was until I heard car doors slap shut behind me, felt the chilled shadows of strangers. Three young white men had gathered around me, their bodies blocking each path of escape I darted toward. "Where does this boy believe he's going?" the one in the work boots said.

As they knocked and beat me to the ground, I couldn't help but think of a boy we all knew of — Tully Jones — whose body had been found some summer before, floating in the river, his head bashed in. When these men finish killing me, they'll drag my body down to the water too, I remember thinking. Please, don't hold me down under that murky water — I can't even swim! Why hadn't I learned to swim? And how would Mother even find my body? What if she thought I'd run off too, like my father had? Up close, the men reeked of peach brandy, the kind my schoolmates' fathers would nurse Friday nights under the sycamores. When those men finished doing what they did to me, I lay chest and cheek in the sand, playing dead, as they staggered back to their car, breathless. Even after they pulled off, sending up a sharp spray of gravel over my body, I kept on playing dead, as if I were sunk down under that endless water, my skin a wrinkled softness that would soon scrape away or be eaten by crawfish, by those microscopic creatures that troubled the silted bottom, until no one could tell or else it didn't matter what color I was.

The following fall, Mother insisted I attend a private boarding school, miles out of town. I wasn't to live in the dormitory with the others. Instead, I woke before sunrise, walked out to the highway, and caught a ride with a deacon from our church, an elderly man who smelled of polishing oil. He was the boarding school's custodian and the only other brown face to grace those halls besides mine. During the school day, we never looked at each other. I was always aware when he was in the same room, but I never let my eyes rest on his, not until we were far away from that place, and even then it was with a kind of shame.

The school's headmaster — the man who had agreed to my admittance — had gone "up north" for some number of years. His surname was the name of the school, and everyone knew it was his family's money that kept that dying boarding school from going under. At school assemblies, this headmaster would find excuses to parade me across the stage — my improbably strong elocution, the sharp crease in my uniform — defiant or oblivious to the contempt my visibility inspired. Even the dimmest boys were clever in their cruelty. Mother had been hired to cook and clean at the headmaster's residence in town, and for this, the others mocked her mercilessly. What could I do, it was true — my scholarship was her bowed back, her bleach-bitten hands. Enrolling me there must have been an act of faith or desperation, like pressing a message into a bottle and floating it onto turbulent waters.

Even so, I clung to my formal education, setting off at seventeen to a small all-Black college, then going far north for graduate school. The boys I'd grown up with mostly stayed rooted. They married girls from church, worked hard to scrape together a living or get ahead. Some were shipped off to Vietnam; a few marched in bigger towns, facing police dogs and fire hoses. I devoted my life to scholarly truth, spending the majority of my adult life here at this esteemed institution. After you were born, I purchased my own home, just a two-bedroom bungalow, but in a good neighborhood not far from campus. I can walk to work, and sometimes I do. Whenever I walk my mind wanders. Occasionally I worry that I've been self-indulgent in my research, somehow selfish in my secret fatherhood. Walking, I think the world is surely a better place now than it used to be for people of color. Aren't I myself living proof against my theories? Can't I be satisfied?

But then, like current, I'll feel it again, even now. It might be the guard at the campus market who follows me when I walk in to buy a carton of milk for my tea. Or a pair of young mothers who push their strollers widely around me on the great lawn. Mostly it's a growing unease about my career. Yes, I was hired. Yes, I've managed to keep my head above water, but in these final years, they've burdened me with the lowliest committee assignments, filled my schedule with 100-level classes, as if I were an adjunct. Of course, this might be a reflection of some defect in my performance — a failure to publish as well as some colleague down the hall, my secret research obscuring my official work. But how can I know for sure? How does anyone know if they are getting more or less than they deserve? All I know for certain is that, last September, a police car trailed me when I was walking home one brisk evening. Me, Professor Cornelius Adams, in my sixties, in my overcoat and loafers, my briefcase clutched beneath my arm. As you well know, cruisers often patrol the edges of campus, quieting fraternity parties, corralling drunken freshmen back onto grounds. They only pulsed their lights at me. When I turned, the one on the passenger side — a Black officer — shouted

23

from his window. Where was I going, he wanted to know. Before I could gather words to answer, a more urgent call must have come in. They turned on lights and sirens in earnest and sped away.

Here are our lives laid out together: At ten, while I flailed beneath the blows of work boots, you flew down a zip line at a well-rated day camp. At twelve, while I reread tattered spy novels on the bumpy ride back home from that boarding school, your baseball team placed second in the region. You brought home a trophy. Your mother took a photo of you lifting it. Eventually she sent it to me.

As you grew older, I continued to make certain wishes clear to your mother — about your friends, your schooling, about the length and crop of your hair. Only once did she truly bristle at my intervention, when I insisted you leave swim team your senior year. The swimming had been good at first, but then you placed at state, a dive so graceful a big-league coach courted you. For a season, you took private lessons, shearing your hair, waking before dawn. You excelled in the water, your mother said — you might get a scholarship or more, so why not let you continue? I could feel her picturing you, her Black son, draped in red, white, and blue, holding gold. In truth, I entertained this vision too, but in the end, I couldn't allow such a glaring deviation. When you were small, I'd worried that you would sink below my ACMs, that you would be dragged down. But here you were, soaring too high for a fair comparison. I did not say any of this to your mother. All I could do was remind her of my unwavering discretion: Hadn't I held up my side of the bargain all those years? When I said this, she hung up on me, and for a long time we did not speak, though I soon found out that the swimming had stopped.

And so I was surprised when your mother called last August to inform me that you were transferring here to finish your degree. I was only startled to hear her voice. I already knew you were coming — I'd seen it on your social media site. Perhaps your return was an act of muscle memory: all the years spent here, at daycare, then later, in the back offices with your mother. It's possible too that you were persuaded by the slick recruiting packets I mailed to your P.O. box each semester. Two years you'd attended that out-of-state school, and while you were away, I followed you as best as I could, though less closely than felt comfortable. Like any parent whose child leaves for college, I was forced to let go of some of my sway — though this gap depressed me. Were you drinking too much, I wondered. Had you gotten in a fistfight, or fallen in love with somebody? I drove up to your campus once but found the whole layout disconcerting — and never did set eyes on you. After that, I watched from a safer distance, monitoring arrest reports, subscribing to your local and school media sites. I hoped to catch a glimpse of your life. Did it resemble the lives of my ACMs, those boys I'd watched so ardently years earlier — their drunken escapades, their fearless hearts?

All I know is, when I spotted you here, you looked so tall, so lithe. I did the math — your age against mine — you'd just turned twenty-one. Whatever else had happened in those intervening years, you'd also become a man. Your visible ease in your own skin awakened something in me. Never mind those tragic stories from other towns and cities, young men lost and taken — they were not *you,* they were not mine. Your ascendance was a glimpse of what could be, and their deaths felt submerged. I realized you had never been average: You were more like a line of poetry too lofty for me to decipher. With you here, I convinced myself that you'd made it out past an invisible trip wire, out to some safe and boundless future. Even if I could not be part of that future, I might still be able to revel in its promise. I was nearly ready to give up on my questions or claim that they'd been answered favorably — those questions of mine, which had always been about hope.

But then — we both know what happened then.

As soon as I heard what they'd done to you, I wrote through that first long night and canceled my next day's classes. Decades of research became a single anguished letter detailing the difference I could now measure on your face. I wrote about the burden of Race — how it warps the lives of Black and white people. I did not speak of my experiment directly. Instead, I used what happened to you as an anchor for my findings. I could never have predicted that my essay would spread so widely, that inside of a week I'd be invited to appear on several networks and a handful of national radio shows. In sound stage after sound stage, I laid out my meticulous argument, supported by data and by events I'd witnessed with my own eyes. I thought they'd be convinced; instead, they interrupted with other stories, opposing conclusions. I thought they might believe me; instead, they held up a few undisciplined lines from my essay as proof that I was angry and absurd. Death threats flooded my in-box, along with crooning love letters from mothers and sisters, from fathers and sons. Still, last night I was contacted with an offer for publication — not from a prestigious university press, as I'd always envisioned, but rather a two-book deal from a large traditional publisher best known for true-crime stories. Maybe there I can finally write what I want — if it's all right by you — about what's been done to me, about the things I've done.

As for what happened to you — I saw the pictures like everyone else, I read every account. I studied the cell phone video, frame by bloody frame. Here is your face, in which I have always recognized fragments of my own. Here is your blood, too bright and pouring. Even as you lie stock-still, pinned to the pavement, the police shout staccato commands, which they seem desperate for you to follow. The camera veers and I see them too, sauntering by in spotless sneakers, their ball caps askew. They look relieved that it's you there on the ground, or else they flash faux gang signs at a camera only they seem to appreciate. The police made a statement before the video surfaced, in defiance of the fact that there is always a video nowadays. You seemed dangerous, they said, and I think of you as a swaddled newborn. They feared for their safety, they said, and perhaps this is true. Later, in a press conference, they admitted you had an ID, but there was some discrepancy. It was from a neighboring state and unfamiliar. You did not appear to be who you said you were.

Beyond all of this, I understood a separate truth, one not yet found in any publication. I knew that they had *chosen* you out of all those wasted students partying on the strip of college bars. I knew this because I'd worked late that night, the first warm evening of spring. I'd decided to walk home through the carnival of youth, and only by chance spotted you out front of that bar on the corner. You were right there in the fray of students, half swaying to music that spilled from an open patio. You tilted your head toward me — did you see me too? Did you recognize me? I can't adequately explain it, but I must tell you now that *I* was the one who called the precinct, claiming to have seen a "suspicious young man" at the corner of University and Fourteenth. I called, but I did not specify your height, your *color.* Afterward, I hurried home, reassuring myself. Nothing will come of this,

I tried to tell myself — and I will finally be able to let it go, or be let go by it. Son, please believe this, if you believe nothing else I've written: This was a test for *them* — for the world! — not for you!

But here, again, we must take a step back, and remind ourselves that this has all been in service to something bigger: that someday our sons' sons might be spared. Your mother used to say to me, The seas are rising, whatever you believe. Soon we will all be wet together, and together we will gasp for air. . . .

I saw you again the other day, out on the lawn at the student-led protests. At first I didn't recognize you, with that white bandage plastered across your head and the new bowed way you held your body. But then they delivered you to the front, the small crowd swelling in support. I've read there have been other demonstrations on other campuses along the East Coast. A rainbow of faces chanting and wailing, as if there are multitudes of watchers now. When I saw you, I knew that you would recover, and it felt like I could breathe again for the first time in a very long while. But even closer to the bone was a feeling of grace that may well soon release me. I mean, look at you — look at all *you've* accomplished, in spite of everything. You made it here, just like *they* did. And I saw you, son, turning and wild — free, even — for a moment at least.

VIRGINIA IS NOT YOUR HOME

They hung that name on you at birth, but Virginia was never your home. Read *Nausea* by Sartre and give yourself a new one. Trumpet your new name to the liver-spotted washroom mirror, like a coronation. Gape your mouth then angle your tongue behind your teeth. While you're at it, work to remedy those other afflictions: that fetid high-hill *r* that has planted itself in the middle of words like *wa-r-sh.* Scrub the stink of manure from your clothing and, while your young body churns over the basin, keep whispering your new, still-secret name. Believe that if you can just change this, you can change everything.

When your furtive girl body begins to unfold, pull your hair back so severely that the boys don't tug you down below the bleachers. Take to wearing Father's faded stable flannels to ward off solicitations to a string of tissue-paper dances. Don't accept it when they ask, *Who do you think you are,* whenever you test some sweet, protracted word on your tongue. Don't accept the moldy hymnals, the marquee salvations — the wayward way that Momma courts heaven like a scornful lover. Don't ache too badly for milk cows in the pasture, their slick contoured ribs pressing through. Take French, lock your doors, and trust in your own sixteen-year-old self.

Fill out an array of applications, but don't tell Momma when you win a scholarship to an all-girls college toward the center of the state. Instead, let the screen door clap closed behind you. Feel brisk air rush by as you sprint barefoot through her hand-me-down fields. Run past the paddock — where your father attends to their cruelest horses — all the way to the muddy creek banks. As breath stings your lungs and a stitch claws up your rib cage, howl victorious into the night sky.

At freshman orientation, chew up and swallow the first name tag they give you: Write yourself a new one. Someday soon you'll make it official, this new and chosen name. Smile with restraint so that no one can question the slant of your eyeteeth — those hidden incisors, white as fresh milk, since, according to Momma, there was fluoride in the well water. According to Momma, she did not expect a dusky girl-child like you, never mind Father's complexion. According to Momma, nothing is promised in this world.

Tell the other girls you've lost both of your parents when they ask why you didn't go home over Thanksgiving break. In the coming months, they'll invite you places: a cottage on the Cape, a brownstone in Georgetown for New Year's Eve. These young women who grouse over dining hall menus, who can't imagine divining supper from scraps. Take note of the weight of their family silver, the briskness of their Black butlers' hands, cuffed in starched white. Take note of the line of first-edition books along their parents' mantels. Read Camus and Kafka to tatters. Read Simone de Beauvoir.

Work harder still and, as soon as you are able, transfer to a bigger school, one with a better language department. Don't fret that it still sits in your namesake state — *Virginia* or *Ginny,* like your one sweet-faced grade school friend used to call you. Those girls you grew up with, who preened in pickup headlights, who got themselves knocked up then abandoned before they reached legal drinking age.

Study your new suburban suitemates but

don't follow them to their beer-soaked parties. Instead, take a Greyhound to a protest near the White House. Lead a chant against the bombs being dropped in a desert you can't properly name. Shake your fists at those suited, greedy men determined to devour the world before you even taste it.

Work double shifts weekends at the rural country club on the outskirts of your Blue Ridge college town. The steep, winding bike rides make you feel like you've hardly left the place that reared you. Shuttle trays to large round tables: gin and tonics, jumbo shrimp cocktails, chicken cordon bleus. Ancient couples shift in three-piece suits and gowns glinting with costume jewelry. All that pomp against your black V-neck sweaters and second-skin leggings, your hair always coming undone around your face. The men ogle your cleavage. A few pinch your bottom, saying, *Smile, why don't you?* Watch how, as soon as their wives turn away, they circle back to lay more money on your table. Save every goddamn penny and buy a plane ticket to Europe.

Ride the trains from Firenze to Prague, from Prague to Munich. Tell yourself, *I am here, I am here,* like a song. Tell yourself here are History and Culture and Power. Here are the old writers who wrote books that you believe saved you. Here you are with your notebook outside a café: If you hold your mouth right, you feel like you nearly belong. Never mind that the cobblestones underfoot recall your steep and rutted driveway, that the hostel's duvets summon Momma's mildewed quilts. Bolt upright in the sleeping carriage at the knock in the night as your train crosses yet another border. Curt foreign voices demand, *Passaporte!* Hand over your full and legal name.

Outside a discotheque in Paris, lean into a striking dark-haired man. He whispers your chosen name to you, his accent making it new again. When he asks where you're from, list a string of cities you hope to soon visit. Tell him London. Tell him Barcelona. Tell him Tangier. Hurry back to his place and allow him to take you — a satisfying shock like diving into spring water. Call out a strand of inelegant *rrrrrr*s followed by a sob of release.

Turn your head, catch the eye of another man, less beautiful, but an artist — a photographer — and from a good French family. Don't go to bed with this second man right away. Stay with him in his family's sprawling flat in the city, rooms framed by velvet curtains, arranged under dusty chandeliers. Stay with him well past your flight, forfeiting your final fall semester. Promise yourself you'll go back and graduate in the spring.

When this man questions you about the States, answer him as if America is a dream you are still dreaming. Close your eyes and conjure vast open spaces and sleepy small towns. Summon cities for him, bar-lined streets, smoky stages raising men with skin as brown as your father's, their bodies curled over snares or saxophones. Speak to this man in French of Art and Ambition, those foreign words rattling around in your neediest places. Flash him your crooked eyeteeth and hope he sees what you mean to show.

Marry this man in nine months' time, a tiny, secular ceremony back at your parents' home. The animals have been sold off or buried, but there's still one near-level field. Tell yourself it's only a handful of days, it makes sense that your husband-to-be needed to see this place. Don't tremble inside those peeling-paint walls as you hear Father's lone voice echo in the darkened hallway. Don't startle when Momma lays a tattered family Bible in your hands. Silver photos chafe between yellowed pages, your own stark and shining maternal ancestors whose lives ended here where yours began.

Your parents look older than their years, their faces creased and furrowed. They refrain from using your new name but also hold the old one deep in their throats. Let the girl from Momma's church scatter petals on the ground. Let Father march you down the grassy aisle, solemn in a dark suit and boots buffed to glossy. Feel how he clutches your powdery shoulder as if to share something through the press of his thumb. Your new husband seems to find all of it charming, even the new A&P in town, even Momma's cola-soaked ham. As you walk with him along the muddy bank, he mimics the way your father says *crick* for *creek*.

Rent a place near DC, just outside the Beltway: A posh agency there wants to represent your husband's work. Tell yourself it will be six months more in Virginia, a year at most. Your husband photographs looming constructions: bridges, façades. He's out the door before the light breaks to brilliance and he works through sunset when the day is nearly gold again.

Metro to Foggy Bottom, to Dupont Circle. Step through the automated doors, escalating up into swampy summer heat. Don't bristle at the homeless woman near the exit, whose moony face reminds you of your mother, if Momma were dirt-lined and liberated. Don't stare at your server at the teahouse, with her closely cropped hair and ebony skin, though her eyes hang on you for a moment too long.

Come winter, Metro to the National Mall emptied of tourists. There you are, a bright dot of a woman alone in a wide gray landscape. Peel off your red gloves, blow heat into your pinkened palms. Scrawl something you remember of your one time in Europe: a story — you hope — of a girl who got away.

Come spring, dredge yourself from a nightmare of sinking to find yourself unaccountably seasick. Your husband is away in Rome photographing famous ruins. Accept that this is your fault, after all these years of brutal care. You've been reckless in the ways you've wanted, as if there was no end to want. As if the hungry burden of your husband's foreign body could free you from your own.

Motherhood presents itself as a dull ache at your center. Your husband sounds ecstatic on the phone: He'll be home in five days, seven at the most. Hang up and call Momma, who gets to sobbing — from joy? From grief? Eat unrolled Ho Hos and fried thick-cut bologna. Don't ask yourself,

Where am I headed now?

Abandon yourself to wrenching labor, break open and birth a son. Eighteen months later carry a girl, a daughter. Choose your son's name, a clever French one, but let your husband name the girl. It sounds like a fine name, the way he first says it, though your daughter soon plucks a nickname from it, perky and provincial. Your husband's career continues to lift, his vivid seascapes lining gallery walls. While his agency flies him all over the world, you are tasked to stay behind and raise the children. Dig your nails deep into your thighs each night but never let the inky bruises show.

Let your husband buy you a house in the suburbs, an outpost from which to raise these fair and fitful beings. Whenever he's home, petition him still. Tell him you could live in Bordeaux or Brussels. Tell him you would live in Madrid. Never mind that already you know his stock answer, that the money is better working from the States.

Insist on a long trip to Europe each summer, though it reminds you of how big the world remains. Stay near La Rochelle, not far from the water, where your husband's mother now lives. His mother who maintains that your wedding was *trop loin*, who dresses in crisp linen and plants dry kisses on the children's cheeks. The whole time you've known her, she's kept the same servant, a North African lady who cleans and cooks and shops like a wife. When you glimpse this second serf of a woman, feel outraged and full of envy.

Those early years are trying: Persist! The children beg you to play on hands and knees. The children run screaming to greet their father whenever he bursts through the front door. Notice the lavish way he lifts them with only a weary peck on the cheek left for you. Jet-lagged, he collapses on the king-sized bed, leaving luggage for you to unpack. Much later, you wake to the light of his cell phone, its blue glow in his eyes and your shared bed lurching to his needy rhythms. Let yourself feel something too, a pulsing sadness, a lumen of want. Even though, before you can whisper his name, he emits a shuddering groan that gives way to snoring.

Notice how quickly the years are unfurling: The children double then triple themselves. The boy is five, the girl is ten, the boy is fifteen. Your husband's gone bald; still, women swoon at his stubbled jaw and muscled chest. You hear him outside, cursing softly to himself below your open bedroom window. That same morning you find

41

a stack at the back of the closet — old, forgotten journals full of your eager, awful words.

Gawk at those futile, straying stories and don't pick up the phone when it rings. Momma's voice lifts up out of the machine to tell you your father has passed. You feel numb and at the same time untethered, as if an invisible cord that anchored you has now been let go. After the funeral, at the stop sign in town, your husband palms your stockinged knee. Believe he is consoling you even when he says, *Shall we consider moving here? For your mother's sake.*

Promise yourself you'll never move back but take Momma's calls every night. Each small thing she says makes its own kind of sense, but taken altogether, they sound outlandish. Your husband has been home for six weeks in a row, his unflagging presence setting all of your routines askew. Turn away when he mentions moving in with your mother, though he makes it sound like a high-wire trick that might well save you. See how he sidesteps talk of his dwindling work, the partial mortgage payments, the growing distances between you.

Put the house on the market just to see what it will bring — what else can you do? Accept the highest middling bid and let your husband call this freedom. Your son, tall as you, makes fists when you tell him. His mouth twists as if he holds kindling inside it. Your daughter slams her bedroom door, leaving you outside of its dry rattle. Press your ear to hear her mewl on the phone to a middle school boyfriend, a person you'll never meet.

Those first weeks back are trying — hold on. The old rambling house is a circus and Momma's confusion, a grotesque new exhibit. See how she stumbles over the children's names — how she acts like a child herself some days. One bleak winter night she wanders off, though you don't realize she's missing till the corded phone in the kitchen blares. Some city-sounding couple is on the line. They must've bought your old neighbor's place. Race down and find Momma in your car's searching headlights, alone in a grove of pine — a flood of relief. Your own shrinking mother, caped in a mossy quilt and spinning, your son's filthy sneakers like rank mittens on her hands.

Move Momma into a nursing home and visit every day. Even though, whenever you walk in, her body seizes with agitation. Take a break, don't go back, one day then another, until a week has passed. That first time you return, Momma grasps the arm of a passing staff member. You hear Momma beg this uniformed stranger to tell her who in the world *you* are.

Your husband accepts sporadic assignments up and down the coast. He drives to Lexington, to Front Royal, leaving you carless and stranded. He shoots portraits and street fairs and weddings, all of it intimate, fleeting. Eventually he packs his cameras away, reminding you he's always loved jazz music. He uses the last of your savings to open a boutique record store in a strip mall in town.

The children attend your old high school — classrooms from which you once plotted escape. Each day they grow less tied to you, leaving longer swaths of your days free. One rainy spring morning, after dropping off your husband, you collect a rustling stack of applications. Tell yourself they are for your daughter, but never show them to her. What could you do here with no real qualifications, not even having finished your degree? Could you be a clerk? A secretary? Could you wait tables again?

Mulch Momma's feral azaleas. Resurrect the kitchen garden that fed you as a child. Fashion raised beds from the railroad ties you find abandoned behind the shed. Eat lunch on the side porch — white bread with sliced tomatoes — your native hair loosed and scraping your shoulders, your face turned to the breeze.

The next time you visit the nursing home, Momma flies up in her wheelchair. She clutches you with such ferocity, it feels like you've only just met this woman who raised you. There are letters, she tells you, in the house. Letters your lonesome and stoic father once penned to you. *Promise me you'll find them,* Momma says, still squeezing. Hold her cloudy gaze. Let her warm breath fog your face.

Rifle through drawers, overturn crates, leave everything gaping and churned. After days of fruitless searching, admit to yourself that you want to believe. Read in bed by ochre lamplight of glaciers liquefying and waves of refugees breaching Europe. When your husband asks what's the matter with you, let your old wounds gleam. Look at him and plead, *Take me away,* though you don't know where there is to go, exactly. Your husband answers you in French, so quickly you can't catch the words. When you ask him to repeat himself, he reaches over and past you. With one sharp click, he pitches the room to black.

After you and your husband separate for good, fill out each application. Without central hiring and background checks, your legal name is required here again. All this time you promised yourself you'd change it, and now it feels too late. As you hurry out of the new Super Walmart, don't dwell on the line of accented girls working three registers in a row. Did they come from Ethiopia? From Egypt? How did they end up belonging better than you in your no-where, hill-tucked town? Balance heavy bags of groceries in the crooks of your arms and pinch yourself to keep from crying. Your nearly grown children sleepwalk beside you, the girl a sophomore, the boy a senior slated to leave soon for college out of state. Their eyes remain pinned to the cell phones they hold, of which you don't approve. These devices were given to them by their father, to keep in touch now that he's moved back to Europe.

Keep moving and look straight ahead when you hear someone call after you: "Virginia! Virginia!" The voice draws nearer even as you quicken your pace. "Ginny! I can't believe you're here!" Feel red heat spread across your chest. Here is a girl you used to know, her face flushed and pretty still, though swollen with age. Let your body twist, let your arms fly up, even as your grocery bags fall to your feet with a clatter.

Lunge in and holler, as loud as you can, "Virginia's not my fucking name!" Roar into the glassy face of the grandchild this woman holds and tries to shield. Take in an endless, jagged breath, then tug the arms of your own wayward offspring. Slam the car doors shut and swerve away to a stench of burning oil. Take in the tableau in the rearview mirror: gaping mouths, your daughter's eyes welling, and all those lost groceries, which you can hardly afford to replace.

Know that they are real, and you will soon find them: your father's letters. You'll unearth them in an antique chest, varnished in mold, that his own people gave to him. Each letter will speak of dull and dogged yearning, each one will be hand-addressed to you. *Virginia,* you'll confess to the foggy washroom mirror, your reflection thicker, age spots blooming on the backs of your hands. You'll look hard and wonder how the time passed so swiftly, how your mark on the world remains so shallow.

Tell yourself you can start again — there is still time! This time, you'll trek a high pass in Asia. You'll sail to Antarctica to witness the great ice cap's weeping. This time, you'll fly to Africa to follow the last wild elephants' run — you've read they have a secret language, sonographic as whale song.

You'll sing them a dirge and kiss the dust.
Lay a humble ear to the ground and listen.

Something Sweet on Our Tongues

We got dropped off too early. Our Mamas leaned long across bucket seats, scraped sleep from our cheeks, their nails like a ragged kiss. As they pulled away, we faced our school, pressed our foreheads to the glass of the double doors, still locked. We punted backpacks while we waited, pitched rocks at the marquee by the road. KNOWLEDGE IS POWER, it read. JOHN HENRY JAMES ELEMENTARY.

We poured out of school buses too, our voices turned up like a TV left to blare. The drivers' threats grazed the scruffs of our necks: They didn't even know our names. We paraded down the wide main hall, limbs loose, toes pinching more than they had the day before. Our Mamas told us, *You're growing like a weed, boy. You've got to learn to do better. I don't know what to do with you anymore.*

Ten years old and already the top of our

school, we knew how to talk to anybody. We hiked our hoods up, refusing to speak. We elbowed into the breakfast line, wondering aloud: *Why Richard Lordly carry all them books? How many different endings can there be? Why Aaliyah and Khaliah forever walking and talking together, like they joined at the hip or something? How come Fat Rod'ney gotta be so fat? For real, no lie — his plate must be piled high every night.*

We said *Rod'ney* like it's supposed to be said, two separated syllables. The first like something fresh gone bad. *Rot* pressed up next to *knee.*

Melvin Moses Green burst into line, tri-angling a muscled arm around Fat Rod'ney's head. He slapped the back of Rod'ney's neck where a strip of bare skin showed. Fat Rod'ney just kept stumbling forward, shoving a tray of jiggling fruit cocktail and milk, eyes teary at the sting but still cheesing. Rod'ney acted as if they were tight, like they were only messing with each other.

Melvin Moses Green was in our class too, but we only called him Moses. In Gym, on the playground, he drew our eyes, a bright brown boy a head taller than us. We couldn't help but see how strong he was: his thighs hard as footballs, his biceps bulging. Moses was the youngest in a long line of brothers who did not come out the house once their Daddy went in in the evenings. In the upper boys' bathroom, Moses called us soldiers, commanding us to lift our shirts. Elbows in, eyes squeezed tight, we braced for the blows that Moses delivered to our ribs, our stomachs. We turned to let him strike our kidneys so hard it drew soft grunts from our lips. He struck us coolly, paying careful attention, like he was trying to show us something. Water leaked from our eyes and caught in our lashes. Afterward, we let our breath out and grinned.

Some days we got to school so late since our Mamas had to work that second shift at the Hospital or Juvenile Detention. Some days we couldn't wake our Mamas, no matter how we tried. Or else we woke up and no one was around, not even out the window. At the corner, we could see the back of the school bus growing smaller, leaving us behind. Our kid brothers, our baby sisters, would look to us like, What we supposed to do now?

Whenever we got to school late, we had to go in through the office. The Vice Principal gave us a stern talking-to. The Counselor asked, *Is everything okay?* The Secretary gave us pink tardy slips that we then flashed at whoever we passed in the hall. Held them up like, Don't even, like, I'm free! Even when we were just a few minutes late, the closed classroom door always stopped us. Through the glass, we could see how everything had started without us. We wished we could be anywhere else. We ached to be inside already.

Stand and face the flag, the Principal said. *Place your hand over your heart.* We pressed the sore places where Moses had slugged us the day before. We recited the Pledge, mouthing or mumbling or enunciating each word. Only Cherida Smith was allowed to stay seated, light-skinned with pink ribbons blooming from her head. Cherida pressed a plump cheek to her desk, rolled her eyes back way too far like Zombie Face was a game she was playing and winning. We knew Cherida had Type 2 so she got to go to the Nurse at the slightest. Plus, Cherida's Ma died back in September. Your Mama dies, they let you do most anything.

During Pledge, we'd check out Richard Lordly: Lord Richard, we called him. We didn't yet know the thing that would happen, the thing we would do. Lord Richard would hump a tower of books, shiny hardbacks and soft, thick science fictions. His family got shipped from Africa, some dusty, hungry part or else why bother coming here? We shrank from Richard's chalkboard-black skin, mocked the funky way he spoke, like a song hammered out in Music on wooden xylophones. During Pledge, Lord Richard might mutter the words as if they were some kind of ancient prayer. Other times he gave a grand salute, his narrow chest stiff, hand sharp at his forehead and heels softly clicking. Richard would be like, *Ah-tennn-shun!*, doubling over, laughter spilling through his yellow teeth. When he did this, we couldn't help but crack up *with* him, even the Teachers. Sometimes Richard would squeeze his eyes shut, sway his arms side to side like a white lady dancing. A moony half grin would pass over his face and we felt sure he was recalling some sweet, rambling story from one of those books he shouldered. We pictured words rising and battling and winning. The Teachers said Richard was "going somewhere."

They had us read printed paragraphs then answer a strict set of questions in longhand. We did their math equations, got some right, but refused to show our work. We swooshed the brick-red playground ball down through the basket and everybody hollered. We chucked it up into the rafters and everybody groaned. We jammed our pencils into the sharpener to hear that long electric whine, to catch a bright metallic whiff of smoke. How much pressure did it take, we wondered, to break a thing?

We squeezed our thighs tight, begged the Teachers to let us go out to the bathroom. When they rolled their eyes, we called out, *It's an emergency!* After they finally gave us a pass, we took long strides around the farthest hallways. We wandered down to the lower bathrooms, pitched the stumpy remains of our pencils into the freckled ceiling tiles till dust rained on our heads. In time, we found our own way back, but that closed classroom door stopped us again. Finally, we flung it open so hard the knob punched the smooth white wall behind, and everybody laughed. Right away we announced we needed help, but the Teachers were busy with everybody else.

Our Teachers were rail thin or scowling or sometimes soft and wide with lipsticked smiles. They wore printed dresses, hung cardigans on the backs of their chairs. We lifted framed photos from their desktops — the pink-faced husbands, the plump fair children, the beaches behind. We thought of our own Daddies then, the times they drove us to the filling station on Fifth, let us sit up in the front seat. Through the open window, while they pumped gas, we caught them looking at us like, I love you, boy, I love you, boy, I love you . . . *Be good to your Mama,* they told us. *Be strong, you hear me?*

We had fresh mouths, loose teeth, darting tongues. *Your Mama's so friggin' ugly,* we said, balling our fists like we were ready. *You don't shut up,* we said, *I'mma beat your head like a Cherokee drum.* We'd been studying the Virginia Colonies.

At the edge of the classroom, we saw Fat Rod'ney trying to get a rise out of Lord Richard. But Richard kept his eyes pinned to the book in his lap. *You so fat,* Rod'ney said, even though Richard was skinny enough that we sometimes felt hunger just to look at him. *You so fat, your titties got titties! You need a dang girl bra!* When Rod'ney said this, we looked him up and down, his soft curls rising like curds in milk, his drooping chest. We shook our heads and had to laugh.

And Rod'ney laughed too, like he thought we were laughing with him.

That one Resource Teacher we hardly knew was standing over us.

You are disrupting learning, she told us.
Go back to your seats. Right. Now.
You need to stop messing with everyone.

They gave us our Free-and-Reduced lunches on Styrofoam trays at noontime. We balanced the weight of berry parfaits, hard pears in plastic bags, and iceberg drenched in Ranch. We figured we had something, but afterward we felt hungry still.

Mateo flashed a fresh bag of Takis and we thrust out eager palms. *C'mon, you know you got more than enough!* Afterward, we licked burning spice from our fingers. We shredded the bag, tucking foil around our front teeth, like the silvery grills our Uncles wore. Afterward, on the playground, we waved bye to Latrell, who'd caught one swaying braid in a joint of the far metal dome like he was straight-up stuck in the jailhouse. We gasped for air along with Aaliyah, who'd fallen so hard from the squeaky swing it knocked all hope for air from her lungs. She flopped on her back on the mulch near the fence with Khaliah wailing, *Breathe, girl! Breathe!*

That was the day Melvin Moses Green motioned us to the half-hidden place by the bushes. He paced up and down our ragged line, his back flagpole straight beneath the no-name dull green jersey he wore. *Y'all soldiers, right?* Moses sang, and we wanted to answer him, Amen! Instead, we pulled our shoulders back, let the sun rain fire on our heads. Moses thrust his ropey arms toward us, then brought them in quickly across his chest like an *X* or a shield. *Y'all warriors, right?* Moses roared, his voice charged and ticking like something that would go off soon.

Right! we answered, our voices high and tight in our throats.

When we answered Moses, we thought of the mud-streaked commandos we watched late night in the TV room when we couldn't fall asleep. We thought of our older Cousins, grown boys teamed up on corners, who had restless, jumpy hands. Crossing our pencil arms at our scrawny chests, we thought of dopey Richard saluting the flag at Pledge. Sweat dampened our chests. We plucked the collars of our T-shirts, trying to stir a breeze.

When I give that signal, Moses said, *you boys know what to do.*

We nodded like we knew.

After Recess, we had Art or Gym or Music. As we filed back inside, we found out we had Library that day. The Library Teacher hovered at the top of the stairs, her face round and ruddy, her hands gripping the rail. *Most of you did not bring your books back,* she called down as we slowly trudged up to her. *If you don't return books, you may not check out new ones today.*

She told us to sit around the browsing tables and stay "absolutely silent."

We scattered toward to the low round tables, the air conditioner churning. Sweat cooled on our necks and faces. Quiet bounced around in our heads. Waiting, we wondered where Moses had gone off to. And was it true that Richard had eaten only one meal a day, back in his home country, like he'd claimed when he first showed up at our class? And was Cherida messing with us when she told us the Nurse always gave her something sweet? Graham crackers or a juice box. A palmful of red Jolly Ranchers. Cherida swore, if she waited too long, her hands would get to shaking. Her head would throb and she'd have to lie down for a good long while. Sometimes she got so hungry, she told us, that nothing in the world could satisfy her. Once, when her Ma was still alive, Cherida'd been rushed to the hospital, as if that deep hunger hoped to take her to some far-off place.

The quiet and wonder echoed around us. We offered up small sounds to fill it. We drew our heads together and whispered. We snatched at tattered magazine pages.

Zip it, the Library Teacher said.

We kept on talking, our voices low.

Lord Richard must've brought his books back or else they'd made an exception. He circled the library, running his hands along the edges of books he'd probably already read. *Zip it, zip it,* he mumbled into the air.

We got to humming then. At first there was one lone hummer, then everybody's throats filled with that bare vibration. Even the girls hummed. Even Cherida, from under pale pink bows. The humming became that song we all knew — it played night and day on the radio. We worked all together, our muffled anthem moving through that wide-open space. Our tongues trembled, but we held our jaws Absolutely Still. The Library Teacher couldn't tell for sure *who* was humming. She lurched from table to table, shushing us.

Somebody coughed and we all coughed: Who were we to resist the tickling dryness that rose in our throats?

Zip it! I mean it! she said.

How you gonna get us in trouble for coughing? Fat Rod'ney countered, and everybody laughed.

As we laughed and coughed and hummed, the Library Teacher crossed the room to get to her checkout computer. Behind her,

59

Rod'ney's face lit up.

That was when Rod'ney broke out singing. Belting out the actual words to the song we hummed. Rod'ney had a clear voice and each of us began to move to it. Even the few kids waiting in the line for checkout. Even the ones who'd been told it was their turn to browse the shelves.

Cut it out, Rod'ney! the Teacher ordered, her tongue catching on the *d* midway through his name, so that it sounded like some other name. When he didn't stop, she hurried toward him, but Rod'ney ducked beneath the round table, popped out the other side still bellowing that song.

The Library Teacher's mouth fell open. She glared at all of us, but no words poured out.

Just then, Melvin Moses Green walked back in from wherever he'd gone off to. Right away, he began to rock to the rhythm of our song. Moses jumped on top of the nearest table, did a couple moves from the video. The table jumped and rippled beneath him, but Moses rode the wave. We could not help but cheer.

That's exactly when the Library Teacher truly helped us fill the shaky, broken quiet. Red-faced, eyes popping, she turned so everybody could see. *DON'T SHOUT!* she shouted. *Stop shouting or else! You all are so bad! You all are in so much trouble!*

How you going tell us, Don't shout, we said, *when you the one shouting at all of us, right now?*

The Library Teacher ignored our question and ran toward Moses instead. He still stood on his table, stomping and dancing and grinning. *Get down! It isn't safe,* she pleaded, but Melvin Moses Green did not look pressed. *You need to go to the office!* she told him. *Right! Now!*

How you gonna call out Moses, we said, *when everybody's up and out they seats?*

RIGHT! NOW! she shrieked, grabbing Moses by his arm, to pull him down or steady him. When she touched Moses, we all quit singing. Our voices dried up in our throats. When she touched him, he seemed to fracture and rise.

Moses flung his elbow free, jumping from the table so hard his feet slapped the floor. Arms swollen, he grabbed and flipped the table he'd been standing on. Then Moses charged right at that Teacher, his chest angled forward in that battered green jersey. His fists were balled but his ropey arm shot back behind his body. We could feel how badly he wanted to strike her. Instead he toppled the nearest shelf. Books flew to the floor. The rest of us had already moved, but Lord Richard was closer. He hardly had time to jump away.

What is wrong with you? Richard said. Like he really wanted to know. Like he deserved an answer.

The rest of us studied our sneakers, the jumble of open books at our feet. Moses stomped on their fragile spines.

The Library Teacher's voice came out thin: *Go to the office, Melvin.*

Moses kept on pacing, huffing air like after finishing an obstacle course in Gym. We would have gone to him, but we could see his balled fists, and we knew their power. The Teacher pushed the call button on the wall, still Moses refused to go.

The Vice Principal and the Counselor came for Moses.

A little while later, they sent him back to us.

We were tired from humming and coughing. We were beat from crawling and cheering and casting our eyes to the floor. We had one last hour back in our classroom before dismissal. Our throats felt sore. We wanted something sweet on our tongues.

Heads down on our desks, we found leftover scraps of foil deep in our pockets, worked the spit-slick surface between our fingers until our Teacher saw and forced us to throw them away.

Five more minutes, she said, sounding almost cheerful. *Then we can all pack up and go home.*

We could not wait to get out of there. We didn't really want to leave.

It's time, our Teacher finally said, standing up near the door in her striped green dress, like the skin of a watermelon. *If you can line up facing forward, voice at zero, I have stickers for you!*

Why you want us to always turn the same way and stay silent, we told her. *Why you think we want your lame stickers anyway?* But we did want those stickers. Even after she'd tucked them away.

In time, we packed our things and made a line. It started at the door behind the Teacher, then wound between the clusters of desks, all the way to the back wall. We clumped into clans, wrung our arms around each other's necks. Khaliah and Aaliyah squeezed hands, like always, but Aaliyah's family was about to be evicted — she'd be gone before the week was out. Moses walked up and down our knotted line, hand raised to slap somebody's neck if he caught a bit of skin showing. We snickered and drew our collars as high as they would go, trying not to flinch as he passed us.

Get in line, Melvin, our Teacher said. *Haven't you caused enough trouble for today?*

Moses jumped in toward the middle, tugging the frayed edge of his jersey. *I'm just messing around,* he said.

When our line looked about ready to go, Cherida stumbled from her place. She held fast to a hot pink Dora the Explorer backpack — the type they sold at Family Dollar. Hand on her forehead, Cherida wobbled like a drunk. *I think I need to go to the Nurse,* she moaned. Why was it, we wondered, that whenever anyone else asked to go to the Nurse, the Teachers shook their heads like they didn't believe us, like we couldn't trust our own pain.

She's lying! we cried. We thought we meant it. *She's trying to make us miss our buses!*

For once, the Teacher did not make us wait for her to find the stack of passes and print the time and date. Instead she held up her hand to Cherida. *You can hang on a minute, honey.*

Cherida's eyes widened.

She took a step back.

She hiccupped.

Let her go! we begged, reversing ourselves,

feeling sorry for everything at the edge of what we thought we knew. *You have to let her go to the Nurse! Right! Now!*

Walk up here, Cherida, next to me, our Teacher said.

When the bell rang, Cherida and the Teacher left the room first and everyone else trailed behind. We were almost through the doorway too when Moses blocked it with his body. He sprang his arms up across his chest, like he'd done earlier at Recess that day. We looked around, to see who was left, hoping not to be the last to understand.

Our eyes all found Rod'ney, who stood right inside the door. He was grinning at Moses like he knew he was about to be in on something. But Moses shepherded Rod'ney out, arm draped around his shoulders. With Rod'ney gone, we were confused till Moses turned back and raised a shaking finger. He directed our eyes toward Richard Lordly, who stood stalled at the end of the line. Richard was squinting at the words of his book, as if he was not there with us at all.

We swallowed then. We knew.

We thought Moses would lead us, but he only said, *Hurry!*

Richard's head was still down.

One of us balled and flung our fist, striking Richard in the mouth so hard we saw a flash of yellow. Richard staggered back, eyes wide like Why, one hand holding his bloodied face. Then all of us were on Richard. Our fists. Our elbows. Our knees. Our teeth. We hadn't realized how hungry we were: We'd never once felt skin so prized beneath our own.

Moses rocked on his heels, keening with laughter. His eyes darting into the hall and back to make sure no one was coming. Richard Lordly was down, and still we kept at it, like we were trying to prepare him for something. We only stopped when Moses called us by our names. Breathing hard, we studied the wrecked boy at our feet. His salt-streaked face. His glassy eyes. A bitter taste rose up in us. Then, one by one, we hurried out to catch up with the line.

BUYING A HOUSE
AHEAD OF THE APOCALYPSE

☐ Scour online listings daily.

☐ Find a house ahead of your fortieth, ahead of your imminent doom.

☐ Never mind that a house is an investment, a belief that things, on the whole, will get better.

☐ Find a house on a hill, set back from the road, a sturdy brick rancher or a quaint bungalow that needs work.

☐ Search outside of Richmond, not too far from the city, since Baby Girl's still finishing art school here. Keep up your commute, rising before dawn to burn up the road to Williamsburg. Never mind the long drive, the lights you've left on, the busted toilet your landlord won't fix, which is always, always running.

☐ Put a thumb on the scale for any location named for (but not in truth near) a broad body of water. Appomattox Drive. James River Road. Chesapeake Way. Try again for that gated subdivision, the one with the outlier security booth, its zebra-ed boom barrier blocking the entrance. That flimsy arm of protection that could shield you (and Baby Girl) from the flaring world. Never mind the dark-skinned guard who wouldn't even let *you* in after you failed to produce the flier for the so-called open house.

☐ Catch the older lady at the credit union, the one with the smoldering accent, the one who makes the loans. The one who reminds you of your own mother, if your mom had been brown and Latina, instead of Black with an Uhura-do, hailing from Carolina. Wear your hair bone straight, a fresh weave with the tight itch of cornrows beneath, like something true but hidden. Tell the older bank lady you're earning more than ever — no need to mention it's a third as much as anyone else in your office, which you know because you manage their books. Confide that there's a blazing-cake birthday close on your horizon. Ask her, for real, what can she do for you.

☐ Check your credit score with that app on your phone when you bolt awake in the middle of the night. Scroll to see how swiftly the Amazon burns. Scroll to see how many hundreds of species have been lost or consumed within the last twenty-four hours. Scroll to see which items you've saved in your cart, primed to ship at your beck and call. Check to see if Baby Girl has written back and make sure your long-ago ex — her father — remains out west, with all those states like a bulwark between you. Scroll through his newly posted pics, a fresh twenty-two-year-old under his arm. Her cherry pout. Her mocking lashes. Her wet doe eyes. Her gaze veers like yours used to, betraying that same ember of dread. Flip the phone on the bedsheets to dampen its glare and stare up at the blackened ceiling. Lift the phone again, refresh, refresh, to see what might have changed.

☐ Watch *Terminator 2* for the umpteenth time, at the gym, on the treadmill, on your cell phone in your palm. Marvel at the heroine, Sarah Connor, a hell-bent single mother voice-overing the end of mankind. Jog faster, noting how buff she's become, working out in the sanatorium in tie pants and a tissue-white tank. The men with the keys smirk like, *That bitch is crazy,* but you know she's just facing the truth of what's barreling home. Imagine yourself like a Black

Sarah Connor, eyes open at least, core strong and ready. Turn up the slope, the bleating speed, and run.

☐ Find a house on a hill, with a wide drainage ditch, set safely back from the road. Look for leaks in the unfinished basement. Look for a master bedroom that floods with light. Look for wide windows that butterfly open onto a clear view of the driveway. Picture yourself framed by plate glass, a doomed goddess in yoga pants, a faux-fur vest, and Birkenstock sandals. A shotgun's smooth stock balanced on your shoulder, angled out to shoo a gang of hungry men past your property line.

☐ Ask your Realtor, in her carmine suit, about the crack snaking through an edge of kitchen tile. Ask her about the peeling paint shutters — could they contain lead? Considering these and other defects, would the sellers lower their asking price? Would the sellers throw in that generator shining in cobwebs in the corner of their unfinished basement? Explain: You're looking for something eclectic, a house with a wood stove, a gravity-fed spring. Don't confess that your current landlord has blocked your number as your basement rental slowly fills with water. Rivulets run like beads down your easternmost wall, and a bloom like mold invades your nostrils. Some nights you wake floating, your nose grazing the ceiling.

☐ Stockpile reading glasses, and dental floss, and royal-blue-topped jars of petroleum jelly — no need to be text-blind, or toothless, or ashy, even as you tumble toward annihilation. Stockpile toilet paper, and ammunition, and that sweet pastel cereal Baby Girl used to love when she was nine. Stockpile Plan B (while you still can) and plant slippery elm in the kitchen garden, along with nightshade and white oleander. Be ready for the emergency inside the emergency, for when the hordes bang against your door and you find you've grown so lonesome too, so ravenous, really, that you rush to let them in.

☐ Unearth Pop's ancient gramophone and crank it until warbled music lifts from his dusty records. His Ella. His Billie. His Earth, Wind & Fire. Sing along with Ray Charles, "Take me home, country roads," as if to mimic Pop's baffling nostalgia for places that never once welcomed him: the VA hospital that put off his procedure until his legs withered and died beneath him. His blighted stumps, the tick of fever, a stench like stagnant water. It always begins with a gasping breath in and ends with a shallow breath out.

☐ Bundle Baby Girl's coarse watercolor papers, along with your gleaned sewing kits and Ma's rust-tinged pinking shears. Try hard to remember that all of it hangs together, how each wavering piece connects or clings on to some other. When you bolt awake to blackness, try hard to divine where the tears will run first and deepest. Picture how you (and your sweet girl, if only she answers) might hide from the damage a little longer.

☐ Look for hardwood floors and hardwood trees, an arbor raising vines. Look for a patch of sun that might nourish a kitchen garden. Turn on the nearest faucet: How long does it take for the water to run hot?

☐ Beg Baby Girl's forgiveness for missing the reception for her first big exhibition, even if you were stalled in traffic. Even if she claimed that it was "fine." Nineteen and still those flush, plump cheeks, the restless way her limbs swing from a black tank top and tattered cutoffs. Her clear brown skin, darker than yours, her hair tie-dyed at the edges. The haphazard way she divides it, twin braids flung out to either side like a Black Pippi Longstocking. Study her old posts for a vestige of hope: her stitched paper sculptures, her swaying installations, though she hasn't updated them in months.

☐ Learn how to build a fire, clean a wound, skin and gut and say grace for a small once-living thing. Practice those old self-defense moves, a series of katas, like dancing. Remember that one bracing hold that extracted a rare look of shock from your ex's features. Sometimes you can subvert a thing by using its own brute force against it — though this might not be one of them. Ask yourself, do you want these last goodish years to be your bitch-be-cray-cray Sarah Connor years; or would you rather go out with the heady extravagance everyone in lit windows along Hanover seems to still be relishing?

☐ Liberate your hair as soon as you are able, as soon as the shelves at the Farm Fresh go fallow and your office shutters its doors. Consider braids, like your daughter wears, or a tufted fro like Angela Davis in her seventies Wanted posters. Wear Birko-Flor sandals with mossy-green Army surplus socks — because, by now, why the fuck not? Because, by now, you may as well be free. Lay your hand on your new luna moth tattoo, the one that young brother at the parlor embossed over your heart. Remember how he set each fine, searing line, how whole moments later, the marks raised themselves like Lazarus.

☐ Vote, but don't expect it to save you.

☐ March, but don't expect it to save you.

☐ Pray, but don't expect it to save you.

☐ Beg Baby Girl's forgiveness for marrying her father when you were so young, younger even than she is now. Beg forgiveness for bringing her into a world where the man who swore to love you set crimson bruises around your throat. Plead forgiveness for her hide-and-seek childhood, the couches you slept on that smelled either of mildew or of smoke. The bus depots and vending-machine meals, though now, in hindsight, it all feels like a kind of training. . . .

☐ Beg forgiveness that you failed to pray or march or vote or work soon enough or hard enough to afford her a chance to own something of her own someday: a home, verdant and wild, that might sustain and shelter her.

☐ Find a house on a hill, while the interest is low. Breathe in, check the listings. Refresh, refresh, refresh.

THE KING OF XANDRIA

Mr. Attah thinks of this exiled place as *Xandria* because *Alex* is the name of his only son, his last best hope. The boy is thirteen, still in junior middle, but Mr. Attah has a daughter as well. Justina works double shifts at the paper store, leaving their flat in drab trousers and polished loafers as if she were a man. Whenever Mr. Attah sees her, a hummingbird quivers in his throat. His baby girl mired in that lowly job, and yet her job has grown superior to his, because Mr. Attah has lost his — although he must not let his children know.

Back home outside of Lagos, before his wife was torn from this earth, when Justina still covered her hair in bright fabric and Alex donned his school uniform: Mr. Attah was patriarch then. He would arrive to work barrel-chested and angle himself behind his polished mahogany desk. He remembers the potted geranium near the window, the one

Mrs. Ibeh would water before bringing his tea. Mr. Attah mourns all of it, the squeak of the window fan even, his oscillating view of lagoon. Now he and his children are stranded here in Xandria, here in this new and baffling place. Justina has grown as petulant and fat as a steer; whenever she surveys him, Mr. Attah feels weak beneath her gaze.

But there is still Alex: his son.

Alex shot up this summer and Mr. Attah cannot help but admire his son's fine new lankness. A line of pimples dots the boy's perfect brown skull where his ball cap perches like a crown. "*Snapback,* Papi," Alex corrects. "Not 'ball cap' — *snapback.*" The boy's lilting accent is fast fading, his new stories peppered with adages that Mr. Attah cannot decipher. Still, if Alex can manage to shine here, then perhaps Mr. Attah can reclaim some thread of dignity, and become the man he once imagined himself to be.

Now Alex attends W. E. B. Du Bois Middle, a school situated in a flock of trees, not far from the highway. Today Mr. Attah stands in the office, still waiting to be seen. The secretary eyes him, perhaps because he's twice refused the low chair pushed into a corner. Instead he paces, pausing to study

the framed faces of former principals —
men captured in stark photographs with
placards underneath declaring the sequen-
tial dates of their tenures. Mr. Attah brings
his hand to his chin and peers at the current principal's closed door.

The office is a harried place, and soon yet
another American mother strolls into it, one
of those haughty working types, who wears
her authority like a badge. The pink-faced
secretary chirps a welcome, hands over a
ledger without delay. The woman kisses her
boy's sand-colored hair and Mr. Attah realizes he has halted in order to stare at this
mother and child, this solemn union, a
frantic dry fluttering alive in his throat.

"Mr. Attah?"

The current principal must have opened
the office door, silently, while his guard was
down, because now she stands framed
within it. All those old bordered men, but
the current principal is a woman, Ms.
Vasquez, whose surname breaks high in his
throat, like a birdcall.

Too skinny, that's what he always notices
first: Someone ought to cook and feed her
thick and hearty stews. She wears a suit —
a skirted one — along with narrow-heeled
shoes. Her face glows a bright tan color and
her hair is suitably long. Today she wears it

in a spiraled bun like a conch shell.

"Come in. Please. Sit."

He knows she will not close her door because of what occurred the last time he was here. Last time they'd met along with some pale ponytailed teacher, a young woman who'd claimed a grand concern for his son. But when they'd finally gotten to the substance of the matter, the raw pink meat of it, there may have been raised voices. Ms. Vasquez might have accused him of behaving "irrationally" — or was it "rashly"? At one point she'd threatened to call the authorities, eyeing him that day as if he were not a man but rather a wild boar in the bush. If he'd shouted before, if by chance his fists had pummeled themselves onto a stray bit of shelving — it was only because no one understood what he'd been trying to say.

At any rate, today he will control himself, he's given his word. Even if they've had him wait and wait, languishing under the row of frames, the whole office reeking of some industrial cleaner that stings his eyes.

Ms. Vasquez composes herself at her desk, crosses her naked ankles. "Have you given any thought to Alex?" she says. "About what we discussed last time?"

Mr. Attah cannot help it — his mind

rushes off at this invocation of his son's given name. He sees Alex at the shore off the Gulf of Guinea, four or five years old, the edge of the boy's sailor shorts darkened from ocean spray. Then Alex again, on the precipice of eleven, cowering in the court-yard after being informed that his mother had been killed. She'd been down in the Delta, visiting her people, and was only by chance in the crowded market when a child detonated a crude explosive strapped to his chest.

In the months that followed his wife's death, Mr. Attah found himself hot every morning, unable to take his tea at noon, still boiling in the evenings when the world had cooled and plunged into careless slumber. To rest his own eyes invited mangled visions: He'd catapult upright, blinking into the dark. Even the ordinary objects of his room betrayed him — the bedside table, the matching bureau, his wife's dressing mirror. She was a regal woman; some evenings, at her mirror, she would hum to herself a tune as thick and sweet as nectar. "Calm yourself now, Papi," she used to tell him. "Your hot anger cannot cook the yams."

After she was gone, Mr. Attah found he could not bear it. A feeling like choppiness, like he did not know what he might do. He had to get away, but where to? When they'd first married, his wife used to say they would move to the States, that she would give him mighty sons. Mr. Attah had decided he would take their real children there now, on a pilgrimage. He had a cousin studying in a place outside the capital, called Alexandria, which might as well have been named for his own boy.

It took all his savings, family property surreptitiously leveraged, several surreal trips to the consulate, and eighteen months before Mr. Attah and his children were boarding a jumbo airliner aimed toward Europe, en route to America. Mrs. Ibeh secured their international tickets, not knowing it would be her last official act. At the outset, Mr. Attah told himself he would go and come back. In his attaché case, he carried his family's papers, all in order — three months, the visa granted. It was only after the plane had lifted that he realized it was Alex's first time in the air. "We fly away over the water like bitterns, Papi," his son had said, sounding too young when he said it, pressing his forehead against the plane's circular window.

Now Mr. Attah realizes that Ms. Vasquez is still speaking; she speaks and has been speaking and his visions of Alex fall sadly away. He only catches the slithering tail end of what she is saying. ". . . allowing Alex the educational services he would so clearly benefit from . . ."

"Yes, yes," he cuts in, voice lifted. "My son, Alex, is special. And brave, is he not? And strong —"

"I'm sure, but if you'd just look here, at this assessment . . ." She extends a folder, which he promptly waves away.

"You people suggest that my son is not learning, but *if* he is not — *if!* — then perhaps you are not competently doing your job to teach him. What you don't seem to recognize is, in conjunction with everything, this boy, this young man, might, quite possibly be brill—"

Mr. Attah looks up to discover that Ms. Vasquez is wearing that look again, fear along with something else. Her delicate ankles have come uncrossed and her hands waver to and fro like those tragic traffic men back at home who try and fail at intersections to direct motorbikes and jam-packed shuttle buses.

Also, he is standing. It is a problem, this inability toward stillness. He was briefly sitting but now he's on his feet, his hands wrung together, the hummingbird trembling

inside his Adam's apple, a sound like ululat-
ing.

"You people —" Mr. Attah begins again,
then cannot find a fitting next phrase. "I
will go, I must go . . ." he murmurs.

Then he is through the office.

Then he is outside again.

Only October here in Xandria and already
the temperature has plummeted. Mr. Attah
hurries away from the school, the cold burning the exposed skin of his face. The sky,
heavy and slate gray, presses in, and when
Mr. Attah tries to gather his breath, the icy
air sets him into a fit of coughing. As he
reaches his Hyundai, fishing for keys, he realizes, with a bitter laugh, that it is raining!
A god-awful drizzle, even though it's so cold
the rain ought to be translated into snow.

He slots the key in, commanding the
engine to turn over. It whines, catches, but
when he jabs the button clearly marked
"heat," frigid air streams from the vent. He
jabs again, instructively — "Heat, damn it,
heat!" — toggling the lever for the wind-
shield wiper for good measure. The frail
arms of the wipers screech across his view.
A meager quarter tank of petrol left on the
meter. Leaning into the passenger side, he
unlatches the glove box.

Two weeks ago, Mr. Attah brought a collection of papers out to the Hyundai, relocating them from his dedicated drawer in the kitchen of their one-bedroom flat. The family's travel documents and spurious cards of identification, his newly acquired asylum petitions, with their tricky quicksand boxes. This transfer happened one evening time. Mr. Attah's daughter had just burst through the door, trilling a pop song he recognized from home. At once, his head began to ache with the birth of some large and terrible notion. He'd rushed outside, only realizing under a stuttering streetlight that he clasped a profusion of papers to his chest. His cousin had sworn to help with their completion, but all that imbecile had managed so far was to lure Mr. Attah to a "networking" supper — all Nigerian men, all from Lagos — only to keep resurrecting his dear dead wife's name, along with the gruesome circumstances of her passing. That, and directing Mr. Attah toward his former place of employment, dirty work that he despised but needed to tide them over. Work he no longer possessed. Outside the apartment, while he still cradled those papers, Mr. Attah's original notion had buried itself in his mind, and he could not recover it, though he sat in his Hyundai a long while trying.

Ever since that night Mr. Attah has kept certain papers, along with a thinning book of traveler's checks, locked in the glove box as if this automobile were his office. He shuffles through them now, locating a printout of his daughter's work schedule, which he collects from her each Sunday morning.

Just now, Mr. Attah would like nothing more than to return to their tight flat and try to rest his eyes. But, consulting the papers, he realizes he cannot. Justina's shift starts in the late afternoon, so likely she's still there, occupying the sofa, chewing her precious sunflower seeds, her feet propped up like a sovereign's.

Before it became so bitterly cold, Mr. Attah might have gone to the pond at Royal Suites, where his old job was. He used to travel to that body of water each morning, after a brisk but fruitless regimen of scouring the area for work, driving from one hotel to the next. The pond at the Royal Suites sits across from a parking installation, and a guest pass is required for entry. But the guard in the booth was born on the continent of home, and this man — though otherwise a stranger — nonetheless waved Mr. Attah and his Hyundai in, even after his disemployment. Almost daily Mr. Attah would follow the black, paved path down to the water, where no one ever seemed to venture but him. None of the hotel's tourists or businessmen ever went there. None of the receptionists, and certainly not any of the other workers in "hospitality": those inscrutable tribes of golden-faced women, from El Salvador, from Guatemala, gossiping in their own languages. After one particularly foul shift, Mr. Attah had questioned a manager: What was principally hospitable about the act of scouring excrement from tile, he'd asked, and when might he hope to be promoted to a more suitable station? The manager, half his age and wearing a wrinkled shirt, had answered cryptically, "I've heard about you." A few days later, when Mr. Attah arrived at the loading dock door, he was told he was being "let go." "Go where," he'd said, naively the first time, then as understanding built up in his body, furiously.

It was time to fly back — Mr. Attah had realized it then. In truth, he missed home, the quality of congestion even, the fine kicked-up dust. But how could he go back penniless and defeated? And even if he managed to pay for their tickets, what was there to do about his expired papers? Would they

85

cuff his hands tightly together at the gate, press his body to the ground in front of his only boy? That day and for a long line of days, Mr. Attah sat on a bench by the pond, watched the fountain gush water futilely like a drowning man flailing. The last time he went, he spotted a brood of tundra swans. In their great migration, they must have gotten lost and mistakenly roosted themselves here. Aloof, they floated, their snowy plumage breaking the pond's scummy skin.

But now it has grown too cold, and the fountain has been turned off for the season. Last time he drove by, he could no longer even see the birds. He imagines they've flown onward in their own tight wedge toward warmer locales, or else been collected, disposed of.

The absence of the swans makes Mr. Attah imagine doing something rash, or irrational.

The place of his daughter's employment is large like a warehouse, lined up between a Chinese takeout establishment and a beauty parlor, the lot mostly empty when Mr. Attah arrives. He parks at the far end, not having the petrol to waste. Technically this is a store that sells paper, but here in Xandria, every retailer brims with indecision. Paper, yes, in all shades and stacked in high reams, but here too are colorful rubber bands tangled into grapefruit-sized masses. Here are clear tubs of hard, salted pretzels — for some odd occasion that he cannot begin to fathom. Mr. Attah saunters up and down each aisle. In this way he can and has killed hours.

At a far row, he pauses to examine the tiny sets of pillows, for under one's wrists, FOR EXTREME COMFORT WHILE TYPING! Or so the label suggests.

"Ah, Mr. Attah! I thought that was you!"

He recognizes the voice at once and turns toward the hearty handshake that will surely accompany it.

"Mr. Kosta!" he answers, his hands already within the warmth of the manager's grasp. The men shake vigorously, almost as if — Mr. Attah feels certain — in anticipation of a brotherly embrace.

Mr. Kosta is not tall in stature, but broad with a king's belly. His face is the translucent yellow of onionskin. On one occasion, Mr. Kosta invited Mr. Attah to lunch — just next door in the Chinese takeout, but still! The two talked easily of politics and business, Mr. Kosta harping on the woes of Athens, where he was born. All the while they sipped tea so scalding Mr. Attah could sense it warping the Styrofoam it waited within.

Mr. Kosta brings his hand to his face, nodding. "Let's see: ergonomics? We have more workplace solutions on aisle seven-A. Depending on what you're looking for . . ."

Mr. Attah feels his top lip perch happily on his gums. His chin dips into a nod. "Yes, yes!" he hears himself saying, though the term *ergonomics* escapes him. "I am finding everything!" he says, hoping that Mr. Kosta will not ask more about what he seeks. Mr. Attah leans in closer. "Is the girl, Justina, working out?" he says. "Does she continue to perform . . . passably?"

For months now Justina has worked regular hours at the paper store. Still Mr. Attah asks this question as if his daughter's tenure is probationary — as if he and Mr. Kosta together will complete her evaluation. Even so, he feels a flush of fatherly pride when Mr. Kosta confirms that Justina is responsible beyond rebuke. "Hardworking young woman you've raised!" Mr. Kosta claps him on the shoulder.

"Good man," Mr. Attah answers, his voice going highish like a youth's. "I think I may be able to procure the rest of the morning off, through lunch, I mean. Would you like — how do they say it here — to grab a bite?" As soon as Mr. Attah says this, cold pearls of sweat erupt around his hairline. What was he thinking? He can barely afford lunch for himself. Or maybe it would be worth it, to sit and talk and eat like a man. . . .

But Mr. Kosta waves him off, smiling but firm. This refusal makes Mr. Attah doubt all of the man's earlier magnanimity: All this time, has Mr. Kosta, in fact, been humoring him? Then Mr. Kosta clasps his hands again, a warm shake like kinship.

"Another time, Mr. Attah," his daughter's boss says.

Some days, there is the in-between time when Justina is most likely on her way to work and Alex is perhaps not home yet from school when Mr. Attah isn't sure if he can go back to the flat or not. This is because he told the boy — and only the boy — that his shift at work changed. This mis-clarification was only to explain why he might be home in the early evenings. But after saying this, Mr. Attah realized that, for almost every hour on the clock, at least one of his children expected his absence. Watching Mr. Kosta walk away, Mr. Attah feels he can no longer stay in the store, nor can he go back to their cramped apartment. He forges a path toward the front registers, commandeers the store phone line, prompting the woman working there to dial the number for Alex's school.

By the time he travels back, a wall of yellow buses awaiting dismissal dominates the front loop. This time the secretary greets him promptly, "Oh, they're waiting for you." She rounds her desk, parading away from the principal's office so that Mr. Attah has to rush to follow, tracking her through a maze of hallways. He keeps an eye out for his own son, but only glimpses the sandy-haired boy, the one whose mother marked him so lavishly with her kiss.

The secretary stops at a door, pushes it open. The room beyond hushes.

As he steps in, a woman's voice trumpets, "Ah, Mr. Attah! You're here!"

Now he can see Principal Vasquez, standing near the center of a conference room. She is flanked by the same ponytailed junior teacher who tried to bamboozle him with claims of his son's shortcomings, all those weeks ago. The room is, in fact, crowded with people, edging around a long oval table. Here are Counselor Hayes and Nurse Calhoun. Here is his son's homeroom teacher, whose name whizzes past his ear like an insect. Here is Alexandria City's Parent–Peer Mediator, along with a school-based police officer, in uniform, whom Ms. Vasquez admits to having invited. Mr. Attah squints fiercely at each person.

An impressive number of people are gathered. *For me,* Mr. Attah thinks, his chest puffing up with the memory of pride.

Ms. Vasquez clears her throat. "Take a seat," she says.

Mr. Attah looks again and begins to understand. These Xandrians — with their badges and titles — have more likely come to intimidate, to diminish. He answers in his most decorous voice. "I prefer to stand," he says.

Then in quick succession, the staff delivers its presentation. They allege that Alex is "immature," "unfocused," all the while their sidelong glances mocking his devotion to his boy. They say that Alex needs support and further evaluation, at the end of which he may receive a designation on his permanent record of "learning disabled." They take turns at the screeching whiteboard, their mounting claims flying at Mr. Attah like shrapnel, peppering the exposed skin of his neck and face.

Finally, Ms. Vasquez offers a conclusion. "This all means Alex is at least of normal intelligence."

"Of course! Of course!" the others say.

But Mr. Attah is coughing now, struggling to breathe. The room has grown unbearably hot, so hot he squeezes his eyes closed against it. In the darkness that follows, a long mournful note invades his body. Not a tune so much, more like the absence of music: the eerie ringing silence that chases an obscene and brutal clamor.

Finally, Mr. Attah hears his own voice rise and shimmer. *"This* is what you have to say to *me?"* he bellows. "You dimwits! You mutton-headed fools! Don't you even know who I am?"

When he blinks his eyes open, he sees only white faces, white eyes bulging. The uniformed officer has taken a step closer, his face blanched and floating above his navy uniform. Mr. Attah presses his eyes closed and slackens his mouth: Today he will not be silenced.

"You mean to demean *me . . .*" Mr. Attah tells them, his voice enormous. "Just because that backstabbing brood of malingerers finds *me* difficult! Who does a thing like this . . . a *child* blowing up a mother! No . . . *do not* touch me . . . No, *you* listen: My son is *perfect* just as he stands!"

Now Mr. Attah realizes he has drawn in all the air in the room. Still standing, he expels it, his heart a bit less weary. A knock trembles the door.

He opens his eyes and here is Alex — *his* Alex — thrust into the room.

The boy wears his backpack hanging limply from one shoulder. His new school jacket puffs around him, cardinal red although he'd wanted black. Also, Alex must have heard the commotion: The boy's head is lowered. He peers at Nike Air Pegasus–ed feet.

"Son?"

Before Mr. Attah can say more, Ms. Vasquez swoops in. She hovers near the boy's ear, speaking to him at a whisper, as if to a frightened animal. That look she'd given him earlier, in his office, the one that came alongside her fear — it was pity. "You know why your father is here — what we've been speaking to Miss Mann about . . ."

Alex looks up at the ponytailed teacher and nods.

"Tell your father," Ms. Vasquez instructs, and Mr. Attah feels the tender stab of Alex's dark eyes.

"Let me do it, Papi," Alex says. "I'm a failure at reading. Math is worse. My head's all messed up." Alex toggles his jacket's silvery zipper.

"Justina's always been the smart one,"

Alex says, and Mr. Attah cannot help but picture his daughter, two small bowls beside her on the sofa, whole sunflower seeds in one and their gnawed striped husks in the other. Justina's jaw working dutifully, and what does she have to say to him anymore: nothing. "Justina says it could be good here," Alex continues. "But for now it's up to me."

Now everyone is watching. All Mr. Attah can do is stare at his son. Alex with his backpack half-opened and papers erupting willy-nilly from its gape. Alex whose shoes are untied, both of them, who has his mother's heart-shaped face. Mr. Attah clasps his own chest to keep himself from reaching out to touch the boy's uncapped head.

"Then I can have seventh period with Miss Mann. But first you have to say okay."

Now Mr. Attah does sit, backing into a cushioned rolling chair, which squeaks and wobbles beneath him. Out in the hall a bell dings. A chain of silhouetted young people blows past the frosted windows. For once, Mr. Attah does not feel able to speak, although he manages one tremulous word: "Okay."

Mr. Attah follows his son through a throng

of students funneling toward the buses. Out front, he tries to hug his boy, but it comes out all wrong, like a dance for which they no longer have the rhythm. Alex backs away, red-faced, and Mr. Attah announces he will drive them home.

"How come you aren't at work?" Alex says, a tuft of cold escaping from his mouth. "Ever, Papi," he adds.

"Ride with me," Mr. Attah says again, but his voice falters, and he cannot meet his son's gaze.

"It's true, then," Alex whispers. "What's going to happen to us?" The boy's eyes flash panic before fixing into a shaky resoluteness that Mr. Attah all but misses. "You brought us here," Alex says, pulling his bag squarely onto his shoulders. "I can get myself home."

Mr. Attah's limbs grow heavy. The place behind his sternum throbs with shame.

By the time he looks up, his son is shuffling toward the buses, his slender back stiffened. Mr. Attah watches fervently as Alex falls in with a group of young men whose profiles he cannot recognize.

Back at the Hyundai, Mr. Attah needles the key in. His heart vibrates in his chest like a jet turbine. He backs out of the space, tires shrieking, and veers blindly onto the highway. No matter the lane, red taillights pierce the grayness, and twice he has to swerve to avoid collision. Accelerating, he remembers his papers, there in the glove box where only he can reach them. If they no longer need him, what must he do — drive and keep on until the road ends in black? He leans hard into the gas. But then, by chance, he passes the turn to the Royal Suites — a flicker of brightness catching his eye. Braking, he cranes to peer down the embankment. He'd thought they were gone, he'd been quite certain, but now he sees them cleaved together, still waiting on top of the water, their fat white bodies and sloped hungry grace, as if they will persist at least through spring.

MY MONTICELLO

I.

We claimed it first, this little mountain. Me and MaViolet and a scattering of neighbors, all of us fleeing First Street after men came to set our row of tin-roofed homes on fire. The men came at dusk blaring an operatic *O say can you see.* White heads rose up from dusty Jeeps and dark hair thrashed in a harsh new wind like tattered flags. *OURS!* the men shouted. Their rifles gleamed as if they'd only just been bought: a megastore militia. Through a hasty breach in MaViolet's blinds, I even saw a boy among them, blond and sneering in a pickup window. Men leapt from back seats, sprang out of truck beds, and rushed toward the faces of our homes. White hands clutched metal canisters, swung torches spilling flames. Bright shouts, the rising haze of smoke — all that and more rousted us out. From our patchy front yards, we saw bodies blur as some of our neighbors charged forward to try to stop them. We saw a teen struck with the butt of a rifle, his temple spraying red. A toddler flailed, diapered and clinging to its mother's hip as she sank knees first to the sidewalk. What we saw in those moments riveted us, and then it set us free.

No plan of where to go until my eyes landed on the short Jaunt bus, parked along First, cloaked in its skin of stars and stripes. MaViolet used to ride those small city buses, which catered to seniors and folks with disabilities. This particular Jaunt had sat out front for weeks, abandoned like so many vehicles ever since the grid went down. A break in a roaring line of Jeeps, and Knox and I ran toward it, tugging MaViolet between us, still in her pale housecoat and slippers. Behind us, I saw Devin sprint out from between two buildings, metal shining in his mouth and on his hip. His twin cousins followed, the three of them gesturing wildly, drawing the armed men's attention.

When we reached the Jaunt, MaViolet lurched to the top step, collapsing into an empty front seat. I slid in beneath the steering column where, by grace, keys dangled. Inside, a group of neighbors huddled along the brief aisle, their voices flowing toward us in recognition. A hush fell when Knox crested the landing after me — my college boyfriend, tall and white, wearing wire-rimmed glasses. My eyes hung on him too, for a fraction of a moment, with me wondering rashly, Why is it we love what we love?

Those men with guns must've seen our shadows in the Jaunt bus windows: a burst like fireworks, a jagged brightness, then I heard a known voice shouting, *Go! Go! Go!*

It was Devin's voice — he and the twins had shot back at the men as they made their way to us. They jumped on the bus and I stomped on the gas, gripping the steering wheel so tightly my palms ached for days. We did not so much peel out of First Street as fly away.

That was the night we came and claimed this place, if not first exactly, then first since this dark new unraveling, when everything has been set free again, the way I see it. Not to mention our original due, denied, dismissed, but still there teeming in our blood, at least in MaViolet's and mine.

II.

The men with fire came in the wake of great and terrible storms that felled historic trees and flooded City Hall. They came after the power failed us and our phones went glitchy and dark in our palms. In those moments just after our cells all crashed, I witnessed a jet and a hospital copter both plunge from a rainless April sky. It was unclear whether we were under siege, or whether the world was toppling under its own needless weight.

In those surreal and collapsing weeks, brazen hordes of students refused to leave our college campus. Some threw rain-soaked keggers right on grounds. Others held demonstrations, outraged that their futures had been waylaid, whatever the cause. For weeks, I remained on campus too, an act of desperation or resolve: my transfer and tuition paid represented so much sacrifice and effort, and not solely mine. By then, I'd moved in with Knox, in his rustic but prestigious dorm room bordering the Lawn. I'd leave only briefly, every handful of days, to check on MaViolet, my momma's momma, who just about raised me. MaViolet lived just a few miles from campus, in one of our town's clusters of public-assisted housing. But after my last visit, when I tried to come back, whole sections of campus had been barricaded. A crew of young men, their faces streaked in our school's colors, hounded me off, shouting and spitting, shoving me back. *But I'm a UVA student!* I told them. *My things are*

100

inside! Knox was waiting inside that perimeter too, wholly unaware, I later learned, of how quickly things were devolving outside his closed door. Later, when I told Knox our classmates had barred me, his gaze drifted, as if he could not quite believe *them* or else *it,* which may have meant *me.* The important thing was, he'd come and found me, at MaViolet's house, after I had not been able to return.

Fleeing First Street in the Jaunt, we barreled by Brown's corner store with its sabotaged pumps and boarded-up windows. We veered at a blighted traffic light and rolled down a long sagging road past small, once-cheerful-looking dwellings. By then, those houses stood battered and grim-faced, ringed in waist-high lawns.

Behind me someone said, *You cut?*

Someone else called out, *Everybody all right?*

Then folks' voices began to surge with new panic. *Is that them? Oh God! They're still coming! Drive!*

It was true, in the side-view mirror, I could see an inky Jeep was gaining speed behind us. More men and the same, closing the distance, and what would they do when they reached us — what should *we* do?

101

Fresh cries floated up from the aisle, but for a moment all meaning of those words was lost on me: A deep ringing invaded my head. I spun the wheel right at the intersection, but the Jeep turned too, trailing at a distance. Now we were heading south toward the edge of town.

Lord, what is happening? I heard MaViolet say.

I did not know where we were going — I only knew I meant to get us all away. I might've taken the exit for the highway, except a lone man was pacing its slanted mouth. When he saw our Jaunt, the exit man splayed his arms. He seemed to be yelling but I couldn't tell *what* he was yelling. I could not tell if he meant to lure us or to warn us away. A bandana covered most of his face, and something dark dripped over and around his eyes.

Behind us, the Jeep screeched to a stop, straddling both lanes, as if there were an invisible line drawn.

I kept straight, my pulse wild in my throat as our hometown shrank and cowered behind us. The voices in the bus went silent again, and in their absence, I could hear the *shhhhush* of tires gripping, an unsteady rumble as we treaded fallen branches. In the rearview, MaViolet worried the yoke of her housecoat, her face caught in waning copper light. I drove us past the community college, where I used to go, tucked into rolling hills. We were fast approaching the rise of the Piedmont Mountains where the road slid between the shadows of trees. At the last failed streetlight, I swung us left, if only to disappear the specter of that oil-black Jeep still spun out across the road.

I did not know that I would bring us here. Not even as we passed the steep drive up to the orchard, or slowed at the curve near the old-timey general store, with its dark planked walls and the massive wheel of the mill clinging to one side. Across a parking lot, a plantation house turned tavern shone white with black-shuttered windows. I kept on, following the slender tree-lined route, rounding a set of S curves, pulled forward as if by gravitation. The Jaunt, squat and heavy, skidded toward the edge of the road like we might tumble into the trees. It was only when I saw Monticello's stone-faced bridge, lucent in the twilight: That's when I understood.

I drove us underneath that bridge and followed the driveway as it doubled back and overtop the same arch. Then we began our final ascent. Slowly. Up and up, as if we'd spent our whole lives climbing. Past a wooden gate, breached by a fallen branch. Up through the towering trees.

We rounded a small loop and rolled up on the welcome pavilion — a complex of stone and wooden buildings around an open patio — as if arriving for some rare evening tour. We jerked to a halt in our lost-and-found Jaunt, pockmarked by bullets: The men on First Street had shot out a set of windows, so we arrived with glass glittering on our scalps.

We were mostly neighbors, mostly brown and Black people, sixteen of us in all. The youngest among us was three months old. At seventy-eight, MaViolet was the eldest. She floundered in her seat, her arms splayed for purchase. Knox helped her to her feet, his glasses speckled with what turned out to be someone else's blood.

We came with whatever we could grab or hang on to. The Yahya family, who had two young children and a baby, brought yards of colorful fabric tangled in Papa Yahya's arms. Ms. Edith, who was well into her sixties, but spry and owllike in her downy brown tracksuit, carried a leatherette book of psalms. The white couple from the white house across the road, Ira and Carol, carried two snowy hens, clucking and bristling in their grasps. KJ, who was slight for ten

104

and on his own, carried a drab pea-green suitcase with a rip running along one side. Our neighbor LaToya — who we all knew sold herself — carried her own gleaming body, her rust-colored hair and near-white skin, her cheeks doused in rose-gold blush.

Among other things, Devin carried a bright seed of angry. His cousin Elijah, who was built like a wall, hefted a large duffel full of handguns and clips. Elijah's twin, Ezra, the smaller of the pair, carried one handgun, along with the smell of reefer in his hair. The guns had belonged to the twins' father — Devin's uncle — who'd been decorated police out in the county.

We stepped down cautiously, testing the new ground.

We came with nine pocketknives, five sets of keys, and seven useless cell phones, which sank like stones in our pockets. Knox carried the same messenger bag he'd brought with him from campus days earlier; it held a toothbrush, a gridded notebook, a copy of Morrison's *Song of Solomon* that I'd lent him some time before. MaViolet carried empty trembling hands, and beside her I held no more than the clothes on my body: high-waisted cutoffs and a navy T-shirt touting the university's emblem in orange. Months earlier, I'd cut a hopeful scoop from the once-tight collar, but standing there, I tried to tug one fallen edge back onto my shoulder.

Three guards hurried toward us from the ticket office, moving together through the thickening dark. Unshaven men, well into their sixties, the trio wore khakis and cranberry polos, the same uniform I'd worn the summer before. Up close, they did not look like guards exactly — more like drivers, or docents maybe, who'd been begged or commanded to defend the historic house. They looked weary though, their pant cuffs hemmed in mud. The shotguns they raised struck me as ancient, as if they'd been pulled off the wall of some exhibit, as likely to jam or explode as fire. One white guard and two Black guards; the white one stepped forward. *Keep driving,* he said, but our feet had already touched the ground, and we'd gotten here on fumes.

Off to one side, Devin raised his chin, his dark locs cascading toward his shoulders. He made no move whatsoever for his gun, though it glowed in his waistband. Never mind that he'd been a gentle kid, and an A/B student all the way through his senior year when he'd been expelled for fighting. Ezra and Elijah stood behind him, with Ezra's handgun threatening only the asphalt

106

at his feet. Still, I don't believe our weapons were the reason the old guards let us stay. One of the Black guards — the one with the Afro gone feral, like a modern Frederick Douglass — looked hard at me.

I know you, he said.

I recognized him too, from the summer before this one, back when the world was bleeding internally but not yet broken open — at least not for me. There were a record number of wildfires last summer, but they'd been far away, on the other coast. There were heat waves and brownouts across the Midwest, and cascading government shutdowns. There was a national election girded by massive demonstrations — hundreds or thousands were killed or injured, they'd said on the news. Even so, last summer and up until this one, there was power. Tourists still turned up, at least in this part of Virginia. I'd rented myself out here for an hourly wage, donning khakis and a cranberry polo like the old guards were wearing. My internship here had ended up being mostly "security," prodding pocketbooks with a slim plastic rod and occasionally driving the shuttle to the house.

At my interview, I did not tell them that I was related to the shining white man of this house, our third American president and drafter of the Declaration of Independence. I did not tug at that barbed connection even though, that spring, someone from here had contacted MaViolet to inform her she was a verified descendant. They'd arranged for a car to pick MaViolet up from town so that she could attend a gathering at the house, along with other Black descendants of Thomas Jefferson or of the people he'd owned.

They want me there now, she'd said to me at the time.

I should say that our family did not need a call from Monticello to tell us we were Thomas Jefferson's descendants. The story of our connection to that man and this place was already woven into the Love family lore. MaViolet had told Momma when she was little, and in turn Momma had told me, like a cautionary tale. *The body remembers,* she used to say.

When I was little, Momma told me about her first visit to Monticello. The whole third grade had traveled in school buses up the mountain, to marvel at Jefferson's gadgets and admire the pristine grounds. As her group waited for their tour, eight-year-old Momma had realized *this* was the man her own mother had told her about. *But we are, for real, kin with that old white president,*

108

Momma had insisted, even after her teacher bent close to warn her to quit "telling stories." *That's outrageous,* her teacher said. When Momma kept on, the same teacher made her wait by the path while the others skipped off toward the front porch for their tour. *Hold it as your own,* Momma said to me all those years later, and I took it to mean, Don't bother with them; they won't believe you. It was only on account of Ma-Violet — some sense of duty or regard she carried — that Momma marked me with my middle name.

Momma's childhood school visit took place before Monticello's board had begun to publicly acknowledge or certify Jefferson's contact with Sally Hemings: that Hemings was not only Jefferson's young slave but also his baby mama, his darker but not very dark never-wife. *Hold it as your own,* Momma told me again in her menthol rasp before she died. I took it to mean, There's nothing left for us to do with that old history but bear it. I figured that was why Momma used to turn her head if ever there was mention of Thomas Jefferson or his posh ancestral home. She would wince as if praise of that man landed like blows on her body. And so, years later, at my interview, I held my tongue. Even though by then they were pushing a special Hemings tour where visitors paid extra and approached the house through the "enslaved people's" entrance. I twisted my mouth into a smile, told them I was born and raised in town. I told them I'd been accepted to Jefferson's world-class university, a transfer from the community college program. I let them see what they wanted to see: a local brown girl made good.

The guard with the mushroomed Afro lowered his gun. When our eyes met, his name came to me. *Mr. Byrd,* I said.

I knew I knew you, he said.

Mr. Byrd announced to the others that I used to work here. *Love, right? Da'Naisha Love.*

When he said my name, that night, on *that* ground, I felt the intervening omission — but did nothing to fill it. *I go by Naisha,* I told him.

The other two guards let their shotguns fall too.

I could feel all those bodies listing behind me, with the house itself still half a mile up the hill. MaViolet took a step and faltered. Knox and I helped her to the nearest bench. Our shuffling advance broke the guards' loose line, and our neighbors followed.

110

From her seat, MaViolet looked up and all around.

III.

We were shaken and exhausted. I saw then that Devin had been injured: Glass spiked along his forearm like bony plates on the spine of some extinct creature. From my seat beside MaViolet, I stole glimpses as he worked to pick out each jagged piece. I hadn't eaten much that day, and my body ached with hunger, but I felt like I might be sick. My thoughts kept leaping back to our homes, those rooms in which I'd eaten and slept and laughed and broken down. To Ma-Violet's kitchen table, pushed against one wall, with its pattern of yellow flowers. I used to sit there to do homework or while Momma ran a hot comb through my hair, right off the stove's red-hot coils. According to Momma, I was tender-headed. I do recall squirming as steam rose from my hairline. Afterward, I would parade out front, my head marked by a giant bow.

I leaned into my grandma's body. *MaVi, you all right?*

Grandbaby, she said. *What on earth are we doing here?*

To one side, I saw Ira and Carol — whose white house was not technically on First,

111

but across the street on a bisecting road — cornering the guards as if to make an urgent report. *They were right outside of my home!* Ira was saying, his white hair bristling. At Carol's feet, the couple's hens circled, emitting a noise like water burbling. *They had torches, I tell you,* Ira went on. *They had goddamn machine guns!*

It's true, Knox said from where he stood beside me, pacing in long pants and a thin collared shirt, faded stripes ringing his chest. *They drove along my girlfriend's street. I counted maybe two dozen vehicles before I stopped counting.*

Madness! Ira said.

Knox dug a water bottle from his messenger bag, took a long sip, and offered it to me. I felt so sick just then — I held it out to MaViolet instead. She liked Knox, I knew. She'd cooked for him when I brought him home in late winter, a roast with chunks of potato arranged around it, lima beans simmering on the stove. Knox cleared his plate and asked for seconds even though he must've been full. Looked like Knox cared for me, she'd told me, and she wanted me to have someone in the world when she was gone. Even so, when she took Knox's water bottle — thick blue plastic patterned with scratches — and drank after him without equivocation, it hit me how much the ground had shifted beneath us, yet again.

Beyond the ticket office, there was a museum, a small theater, a café, a gift shop. There were other spaces on a lower level — a children's area, a conference room — but we didn't venture into them that first night. The café had been well rifled through, but the gift-shop tables looked pristine, pyramided with books and swanky souvenirs. We telescoped our hands against the glass, peering deep into those dark, unspoiled spaces. We walked the covered perimeter of the courtyard, collapsed onto benches, staring into the centerpiece of shrubs.

The other Black guard — Georgie — kept saying the same thing to Mr. Byrd, tugging on the older man's shoulder. Turned out Georgie was only midway through his fifties, with light brown skin and a low sack of a belly, his cranberry polo folded neatly beneath it. *But they aren't supposed to be here,* Georgie said.

Even so, Mr. Byrd, along with the white guard, Mr. Odem, brought us water and warm root beers and orange sodas for the children, their rifles drooping from duct-tape straps. They brought us bags of chips too, some pricey brand I'd never seen before. They surrendered these items stiffly,

113

as if their hospitality was an old habit, one they hoped to soon be free from. I let a chip dissolve on my tongue, spice peppering my throat. Mr. Byrd opened our glass bottles with a tool that hung from a set on his belt, and offered Devin ointment for his arm.

No one, not even Elijah or Ezra, talked about hiking the half-mile path to the landmark house — not that first night. The Yahya parents arranged a nest of bright fabric near the entrance of the museum for their stunned-looking children, a girl and a boy, six and seven: Imani had on a simple cotton dress, while her brother, Jobari, wore a tiny patterned shirt that mimicked their father's. The white-house couple let their hens loose in the plantings of the courtyard, with Carol — in her clopping sandals — hovering and listening for their alien coos beneath low leaves. Later, the couple sat side by side, gulping from a bottle of magenta-colored wine lifted from Ira's leather satchel, with Carol sobbing stridently.

Devin, who wore all black that night except for umber boots, had found a broom and was sweeping chunks of glass out the back door of the bus and into a bed of shrubs. I saw Knox start toward the ticket office — if I'd known where he meant to go, I would have reached for the skin of his polo, to coax him back. Instead I watched helplessly as Knox approached Devin just outside the Jaunt, and offered to help sweep the glass. Devin waved Knox off, hardly looking up from his work.

You're bleeding — let me do this, Knox was saying.

Devin balanced the broom handle against the Jaunt, looked Knox up and down.

Who are you, man, I heard Devin say, even though he had to know by then who Knox was to me. *Why are you even here?* Devin said. Still Knox reached out as if to take the broom in his hands. A shudder ran through Devin's body; his mouth flew open and I caught a second glimpse of his golden crowns, which I'd only ever seen before that day by surprising him into laughter. Knox opened his mouth too, to answer, but Devin squared his body, like he might strike Knox. Don't, I wanted to say. I wanted to shout something protective between them. Before I could say anything, Devin punched the side of the Jaunt hard enough that the metal rumbled. Knox backed away, his hands slightly raised, and Devin dug a Zippo from his pocket, lit a cigarette. Then Devin began to sweep again, the glass against pavement making a fractured sound.

Thing is, Devin and I used to go together, the summer before I started high school, back when I was like, *Go Black Knights!* That was a few months after Momma died, leaving a massive hole at my center like something sacred excavated. We were just kids, thirteen and fourteen, and Devin would walk with me to Brown's corner store, where we'd buy wings and potato wedges out from under the yellow heating lamps. He'd open the red-and-white-checkered box between us, the puff of fragrant steam, everything fried and salty and glistening with oil. Puppy love was all it was, though we played at being grown. We only hooked up once, in his small basement room, at the tail end of summer. I was living with Ma-Violet, and Devin was staying with Ezra and Elijah and their father. Having sex when we were so young ended us. Later, I understood I was hardly ready. Much later, he admitted he hadn't been, either.

I met Knox last fall during my first semester at the University of Virginia. He was — I later learned — a fifth-year and a fancy honor student, but I didn't know that when we met. I only knew he was the only white boy to come to the first of our Students for Equity meet-ups. I'd volunteered for outreach and so he'd come to my table to get his HELLO MY NAME IS. *I'm Knox,* he'd told me, stooping close so I could hear him, asking my name too, then carefully repeating it. With him in Engineering and me in Education, that might have been the end of it, except I've always struggled with numbers, with probabilities. When I reached out at student services for support, there he was again, his light eyes looking bereft somehow behind glass and wire. I was drawn to the stark angles of his face, the focus he set. I'd been told a couple times in high school, "You're pretty for a Black girl," but in Knox's expression, I saw no such qualifier. In the tutoring sessions that followed, we'd sit on separate blankets on the Lawn, beyond the shadow of the rotunda. Sometimes Knox would look at me as if I were as familiar as water. One day he brought a photograph to show me: his family, out in Washington State, posed in front of a mountain lake, the water a faceted blue-green, like a gemstone. In the photo, his father looked austere in a flak jacket and flannel. His mother stood near Knox, handsome and blond, her eyes the same non-color as his. His younger brothers crowded together, bare chests streaked in mud, their thin arms linked. *I haven't been home in a while,* he'd told me as I studied that picture.

He picked a red leaf from the river of grass separating our blankets. Then Knox said my name, like a question. One that I understood. One I'd already been asking myself.

Later, after we'd gotten together in earnest, after the air had grown cold enough to draw frost from our words, Knox and I took a giddy selfie on the Lawn, our bodies angled close. I felt short, of course, nestled there in the pit of his arm. Knox smelled like castile soap and wood smoke, since it was finally cold enough that he'd begun to use the fireplace in his dorm. I remember I could feel him peering down at the crown of my head with such adoration, my hair pulled taut to a puff at my neck, a bind that he would undo that same night with trembling, reverent fingers. Posing there, I knew there was nothing so peculiar between us, between *any* one person and the next. But when we looked at the result, we had to pretend it wasn't a jab, the way the flash could hardly contain us — it blew out Knox's fine features and burned mine to pitch.

What I mean to say is that I love Knox — I'm *in love* with him, even if something happened early on in the unraveling. It happened during spring recess, before the planes fell, when Knox flew back to his home state and left me in mine. I went to stay at my room at MaViolet's, planning to escort her by bus to one of her doctor's appointments. Her pulmonary specialist was at the university hospital, and they'd kept switching up the date for her visit, everything already falling apart, though we had no idea at the time how far it would fall. When we arrived, they explained a change in policy: After that visit, unless we could afford to pay in full, we should make other arrangements. On our way out, a nurse stuffed a plastic bag with emergency inhalers and handed it me.

That evening, back on First Street, I must've been feeling low. I spotted Devin out the family room window. It had been such a long time and it felt *good* to see him. I slipped outside, the screen hinge whining softly behind me. I knew Devin had been through some things since I'd last seen him, but as we walked together — out past the ball courts with netless hoops and the wild greens of the community garden — we only talked about the old days when we were just kids on that same stretch of road. The way we talked that day, the pain of the past felt like a kind of pleasure for the simple fact that we'd shared it between us. Devin lit a cigarette and that smell reminded me of

Momma. We kept on, all the way to his uncle's place, all the way to his room, remembering every little thing.

What can I say except *The body remembers.* Momma used to always warn me to be careful, as if my girl body was a ticking time bomb. And I was careful — I *had* been. But just then and into the early stages of the unraveling, with all the closed offices and unstocked shelves, I'd failed to be careful, even with Knox. Spring recess ended and I went back to Knox, because we'd promised each other *I am yours and you are mine.* I went back to campus, to the life I'd been striving for, because I wanted to, even if those slow, unspooling moments with Devin had moved me, like reading a passage in a forgotten book, and finding — in those known words — a revelation. I went back, telling myself that what happened with Devin had been a misstep, or a sidestep, something to be buried. Then came those monumental storms, all that wind and water, and it was only afterward that I realized.

Devin knows about Knox, but Knox doesn't know about Devin, except for our pre–high school romance, which is ancient history. No one in the world knows that I'm pregnant — except for maybe MaViolet, who might see me more vividly than I can see my own fool self.

While Devin cleared the broken glass, Knox walked back to me. He was shaken, I could tell, by Devin's anger and by what had happened that day on First Street and all the days that led us to it. I had MaViolet right beside me, but Knox's family lived across the country — he couldn't even call to see if they were okay. I knew that when Knox had flown home for spring recess, his father had refused to look at him. His mother baked bread and set the table, but only spoke to him sparingly, about small things. Even his younger brothers sat on their hands, as if they'd been instructed to leave him untouched. In high school, Knox had begun to fall out with his father after the older man had had some sort of epiphany, or crisis, abandoning his networker job in Seattle and relocating the family far north to live off a wild rocky plot of land. Knox told me it was because he'd challenged his father's new vision of what the world was and should be. It was because Knox had insisted on leaving for an elite East Coast college. It was because, just before winter break, Knox had told his parents that he was seeing someone. He'd sent them *my* picture, from his phone, the one with overblown darks and lights.

I was up on my feet before Knox reached me. He bowed to press his forehead to mine. *Da'Naisha,* he said.

I understood then that Knox was apologizing for *all* of it. For the failing world that we'd both inherited, but a world that he'd been assured, in winks and nods, was his birthright and endless domain. For those men with skin the same color as his, who had terrorized people with skin like mine. I looked down at my sneakers, at the angled mosaic of bricks beneath our feet.

My whole life, it seems, there's been a revival of hatred and violence toward people who look like me. Waves of men have surged into our town from all over the state, the country. As girls, we all heard about the young white woman killed by an outraged white man who sped his car into a crowd of marchers raising signs in our defense. Even though my momma'd warned me not to look, I snuck the video so I could see with my own eyes. The white man's dark car screeches in, sending up a flock of broken bodies. I watched a second time, in wonder, as if by careful study the damage might be undone. Weeks later, waiting at a bus stop with Momma, I overheard two white ladies going back and forth about it. The lady with the rain scarf knotted at her chin claimed that the recently dead girl had not, in truth, been killed by any car. The photo on the news was dated, she said, and the dead girl had gotten fat since it was taken. The other lady, who was heavyset herself, with a face like bread dough, bobbed her head. She'd heard the fat dead girl had died of a heart attack, in the middle of the protest, right there on that road not far from where we were sitting. I tugged the weary skin of Momma's arm, willing her to set them straight. But Momma just kept looking down Main for a bus that wasn't coming. I took all this to mean the slain girl's lush body was a ticking time bomb. I took it to mean that young women could die of wanting too much.

In the years that followed, the men came again and again.

As I got older, whenever the men came, MaViolet said, *Hold your head up,* in a way that sounded like *Be careful.* My girlfriends groaned softly or flipped on their phones, reminding me of how Momma used to do. Folks on First snatched their kids back in before dark and murmured from plastic lawn chairs on their stoops some version or another of *Here we go again.*

I made it to the University of Virginia, and

123

the men kept coming, wielding bright new rage. Floodwaters rose along Virginia's coasts, but their frenzy remained focused on something about me, something involuntary and inescapable and mine. It was not unusual to see their shiny procession on the strip next to campus — dark SUVs awash with flags, driving at a crawl — still it startled me every time. Once, walking back from the ATM to check my balance, I noticed that the sidewalk was newly littered with clear plastic baggies. Bank receipt in one hand, I used the other to lift a bag, weighted with pebbles, and unsheathe the flier in it. **EXPEL THEM FOR THEY CANNOT MAKE WHITE BABIES**, it read, and there was a drawing of an impregnated Black woman, all belly and booty and titties and lips.

YOU ARE WORTHY, it read, on the other side.
YOU ARE NOBLE!
YOU ARE UNDER THREAT!
YOU MUST NOT RETREAT!
EMBRACE YOUR HERITAGE!
And there was a drawing of a white woman swaddled in an American flag.

Some people saw the fliers and said, *It's nothing.* Some said, *Ignore it, and they will go away.* Some people said, *Fuck you for feeling safe enough to ignore it. Ignore it and it will grow.* I folded the flier to thickness, pressed it deep into my pocket.

The night we arrived at the welcome pavilion, Ms. Edith perched in a café chair, running her crooked finger along stanzas of Scripture. LaToya cast off her foamy flip-flops, her toenails a chipped platinum and shining like tiny shells. KJ skulked near the Jaunt, dragging his suitcase, a thin scar on his forehead arching like a second brow, giving his young face a look of near-constant wonder. Later I learned he'd been sleeping inside the abandoned Jaunt, back on First Street. His mother was incarcerated; he'd run away from foster care.

Devin, Ezra, and Elijah set up café chairs along the loop and sat peering down at the entrance road — their own handgun vigil, separate from the old guards' patrol. Only Georgie, with his high voice, protested: No one but us had come here, he warned. How could *we* be guards, when we ourselves were the trespassers? His critique did not stop Devin or the twins, though I wanted to echo my own misshapen version of it. Aren't we safe enough all the way out here? I wanted to say. I'd figured that we'd drive back that night, but as folks began to sprawl onto benches, I had to face the truth. I asked Knox to help me make MaViolet more comfortable. We found a sheltered place under the covered lip of the patio and sat her up in a wooden chair padded with spare clothes, propping her stockinged feet up in a second chair. We lay down too, not far from her, but in the open, out on shade-stunted grass. We did not have a sheet below us. Our heads lolled on Knox's messenger bag. It was still spring but that night, like those before it, felt fevered. We hoped, in that small clearing, to catch some sort of breeze.

What are we s'pose to do, I heard myself say.

Knox wove his long fingers in between mine. *What can I do for you?*

I turned onto my side, facing away from him and down the slope, where smaller trees huddled. The moon that night was full, the ground pearly with its reflection. Our hands still bound, I tugged Knox's arm around me, trying to temper the separation between our bodies. I thought of the candle burning into a puddle in the windowsill of MaViolet's bathroom. The night before, I'd stood in its flickering light, checking for blood. The clasp of Knox's messenger bag bored into my cheek.

Could you make me not be knocked up, I

thought.

I'm all right for now, I said.

I ran my free hand over my belly, which was flat, but for how long? Understand, I wasn't ready to be pregnant. I wasn't sure if I would ever be ready. Even before the unraveling, with the world as it was, I'd set my sights on bounded things: I wanted to get my degree, to go to grad school, maybe. I wanted to become a teacher, to do something for somebody the way so many people had done for me.

Are you sure? Knox said.

Could you make this baby yours, at least? I thought.

I couldn't be sure if Knox was the father, or if Devin was the father. I pressed into Knox's body, looked up at him from under his chin, and offered my mouth, even if the whole cavity of my heart ached. Knox kissed my lashes, the blunt slope of my nose. He ran our still-joined hands up so that his thumb brushed my rib cage, my chest, until the sound of wanting him escaped my parted lips, despite my deep worry. He kissed me slowly, studiously. He cocooned his body around mine despite the heat. We stayed like this, turning in tandem, trying to spare our hips, our shoulders the unrelenting hardness of the ground.

When I felt Knox drift into watery sleep, I untangled myself to lie on my back. The ground felt uneven and endless beneath me. The moon shone high and bright in the patch of open sky. I could hear MaViolet's soft snoring cut through the chirp of insects.

I was so tired my eyes burned, but when I let them close, all I could see was the slant view from MaViolet's window: men with guns rushing forward, their faces glinting orange, reflecting oily flames. That one pale boy in the pickup window, all hair and teeth. In my head the boy was grinning fiercely, his thatched hair an ashy blond as if it were an extension of his skin, his eyes protruding in ecstasy or terror. My eyes flew open. In sleep, Knox had thrown his arm back over me. He mumbled something that sounded like my name. Then MaViolet called to me in earnest.

Grandbaby, she said.

I tried to answer. I struggled against gravity to wake myself, to pull my body upright, failing at first. It felt like that bit of earth was trying to claim me, as if I'd been lying on that patch for more than a hundred years. I swear I could feel roots clutching, rocks cleaving between the blades of my shoulders.

Nay-Nay, she said.

I willed myself up and made my way to her, propped in those chairs. In my haste to offer her water, I tipped the plastic bottle too quickly. Water dripped from her mouth, beaded along the quilted smocking of her housecoat. Together we fumbled to brush it away before it sank in.

You think they got to ours? MaViolet said.

When she said this, I could almost see MaViolet's front room, her looming shelving unit crowded with a lifetime of collections: dust-speckled pictures of her late husband, Papa Alred, in his porkpie hat and suspenders; Momma's orphaned ebony African heads alongside MaViolet's gleaming porcelain figurines — everything jockeying to be seen. All the versions of that same front room in the homes of our neighbors, dwellings bridged together in sets of two or four, helmeted in stray slopes of metal roofing as if the whole project had been conceived from remnants. Over the years, MaViolet had lived in three different units. She'd moved from Rose Hill after Papa Alred died and her landlord steepened the rent. MaViolet had been famous back then, for her fruit pies and red velvet — she'd catered events around town and out into the county. But when she looked to rent or buy her own place, she was deemed unqualified, even after she found work in food services at the university. Eventually, she and Momma moved to First Street, a community full of Black and brown people, back when the buildings were newish and varnished in some kind of promise.

MaViolet sat up straighter, wiped her mouth with her hand. *You think they burned ours down?*

I don't think they got ours, I said. I hoped this was true.

Around the way, we could hear Mama Yahya — she was singing to the baby, she was pleading with the baby. She was weeping.

IV.

We woke to the sharp sounds of birds crying. We woke glazed in sweat, our limbs newly speckled in bites from unseen insects. Our stomachs rumbled and our chests ached with all the losses we'd inventoried that first long night. Papa Yahya had left an amber-beaded necklace; it had long ago belonged to his mother, a difficult woman. Elijah had left a rubied ring, which had been given to him by a scout years earlier; the ring had turned out to be worthless, but its gleam and tight fit had inspired a feeling of possibility. LaToya'd left her GED certif-

130

icate — she could picture it, she said, in a top drawer, among loose bills. Ms. Edith had left a small wooden cross hanging on the wall above her bed. I'd left something precious back on First Street too, but I hid its absence from myself until whole days had passed. We woke wondering: Had our friends and neighbors made it somewhere safe? Had we?

The white-house couple had lost one of their hens during the night, so we woke to Carol's shrill call. She would not let up until she found the bird pecking and shitting in the dark aisles of the small theater. Once up, we learned that the white guard, Mr. Odem, had taken off in the night. According to Mr. Byrd, he'd left with one shotgun, driving off in Mrs. Dandridge's second car. Mrs. Dandridge, he told us, was Monticello's acting president. She'd attempted for some time to keep the grand house and gardens tidy, to keep the lights on by way of generator. She'd wanted to be poised to reopen Monticello's doors as soon as the world was mended enough to once again buy tickets to the past. But eventually, Mrs. Dandridge had left too, in her Range Rover with her two bullmastiffs, to be with her grown children outside of Richmond.

MaViolet and I used the dim restrooms

— the faucets no longer worked, so we rubbed sticky soap into our palms. Just after MaViolet had settled on our first bench, I heard shouting. Looked like someone had raided the gift shop during the night, knocking over a pyramid of dark chocolate bars and leaving scattered scraps of gold foil and parchment wrappers. When I ventured inside, I found Georgie, arms crossed, standing over KJ — KJ hugging his green suitcase fiercely, with scrawny arms. Mr. Byrd had come too, his salt-and-pepper hair flattened on one side from however he'd rested. Together the old guards told KJ he best open up his bag, Mr. Byrd's voice appeasing where Georgie's went bright and trilling. *It's mine,* KJ answered, backing between display tables, sweat trailing through tufted curls.

Ezra must've heard the commotion. He blundered over in his long denim shorts, his head spangled in naps. Ever since their father passed, we'd all witnessed his brand of grief around the neighborhood: how he stayed on the corner at all hours, voice too loud and tinged in fretful sorrow, fists balled as if ready to fight. Now Ezra settled those restless hands on KJ's narrow shoulders. *Y'all need to leave Little Man alone,* he said. *That could've been anyone.*

As the day's heat rose, we gathered in the patio space outside the café, clustering tables, sharing what little we had in our bags, rechecking our emptied pockets. Knox scratched out something in his gridded notebook and LaToya took a nap curled up on a bench in the sun. Ms. Edith read aloud to herself and beckoned Georgie — whenever he passed — to bring out more waters or something for folks to eat. Papa Yahya made a series of counting games for his children: How many columns could they count between him and the ticket office? How many doors and windows? How many shades of green?

When Devin approached our loose group on the café patio, his face looked softer than it had the night before, with stubble spotting his cheeks. The twins soon followed, talking back and forth between themselves. Elijah had a voice like a brook, a bulldog face, and a scruffy beard that had once been immaculate. He was the bigger twin and had played a single season of college football. Where Elijah was wide, Ezra had a ranginess to him. The twins looked like brothers, but not like the same person, as if one began where the other ended.

The Lord is my strength and my shield, Ms. Edith said.

Ira sank into a café chair as if he were melting. He'd cast off his blue button-down, revealing a bleached undershirt, white hair spilling from the deep V. He had been a lawyer once, a dogged do-gooder who took on lost causes and paid a hefty alimony — hence his retirement near our cluster of government-subsidized homes. *Where the hell were the city officials,* he was saying. *The goddamn firefighters, the police?*

Carol nodded to the rhythm of her husband's rant, while at the same time swatting mosquitoes.

Police, Ezra said. *Naw, we need to go back ourselves, find those motherfuckers, and make them pay —*

Run on back, sonny! Ira's snowy hair was shellacked in sweat. *They'll see you coming from a mile away.*

Somebody's gonna pay, Ezra said.

Devin agreed, his voice hedged: Someone would.

As if to demonstrate, Ezra then Elijah hopped up, put their dukes up, bobbing and weaving, a spray of sweat flying from their jostling bodies, like they aimed to box those armed men into submission.

Bring it down! Papa Yahya said. *You are frightening the children.* Indeed, Jobari and

Imani stood mutely behind Mama Yahya, who rocked the baby, her thick curves held in pattern.

Naw, I mean to go back, Ezra persisted, cleaving himself from our small congregation, reminding us that we were no group at all, but only sat together on that patio by terrible circumstance. LaToya sat with crossed ankles in a lone café chair near Ms. Edith, digging an itch from her full amber hair. She'd scoured off her gilded makeup in the night, revealing a face partitioned by freckles. *Could be our houses're burnt to the ground by now,* LaToya said. *Where exactly are we s'pose to go back to?*

She's right, Knox said, his voice startling me. He'd pulled up a chair on the other side of MaViolet. When he spoke, it hit me, along with a pinch of bitterness: Knox probably could go back to town if he wanted, back to campus and to his dorm room.

But he hadn't gone back, I reminded myself.

Slowly, Knox began to chart the dimensions of our predicament, calling on the old guards to answer his questions. Mr. Byrd had a working vehicle, a Lincoln Town Car, parked in the lower lot. And in addition to our battered Jaunt, one of the older shuttle buses had some gas in the tank.

Where else could we go? Knox said.

I thought of a day, weeks earlier, when I'd walked across campus to Beta Bridge, with its low guardrail wall covered in generations of student graffiti — exposed layers of paint peeled back in places, looking like sedimentary rock. I'd stood alone watching lines of cars leave town, burdened with luggage strapped to rooftops. In the midst of the storms there'd been a hunkering down, but afterward, people pooled what they had and made their choices to stay or go.

Knox looked around, jotted something in his notebook. *But how safe will the roads even be,* he was saying.

Devin had knotted his locs high and messy on his head. *Who put him in charge,* he said, looking around at all the neighbors he knew.

In a way, I agreed; even so, I spoke up. *Let him talk,* I said. *We've got to let everybody talk, at least.*

Knox kept on, telling everybody else what he'd already told me about traveling from campus to MaViolet's house days earlier: how perilous town had looked and felt as he'd jogged through it. Neighborhoods either cleared out or marked by signs warning strangers away. Main Street had been deserted, except near the old bus station where he'd passed a platoon of women wearing dingy white clothing, carrying red satchels. They'd asked if he needed food assistance, medical assistance, their collective attention intense but passing quickly over him once he'd declined.

As Knox finished talking, other folks took turns telling and retelling what they'd experienced on First Street the night before. The hissing insistence of "The Star-Spangled Banner." The way the men had moved in rough formation, like soldiers on TV. *They were pouring petrol at the doors and the wood around the windows!* Papa Yahya said, his voice breaking. *So that the people could not get out, I believe. We were grabbing the children so fast!*

They gonna come up here and kill us! KJ said.

Devin peered back at the Jaunt, then over to Mr. Byrd. *If we go up higher, can we see town from here?*

You're not supposed to go in the house, Georgie said, but Devin cut in: *Nobody's even talking about that house — I just wanna get somewhere where I can see.*

Mr. Byrd said you could probably see town, if it was clear, if you walked up the hill toward the upper shuttle-bus stop. You could see some of the taller buildings on

Pantops, rooftops breaking through the trees. You could see more if you hiked up the zagging path to the adjacent hill, Montalto, about an hour's hike there and back. It wasn't long before a group started toward that higher peak, Devin walking out in front, his head the tallest, with Mr. Byrd beside him, a makeshift walking stick under the older man's fist. The twins went too, along with KJ, who galloped behind, looking lighter without his suitcase. I did not see it on the patio; he must've hidden it.

Knox and I remained at the welcome pavilion, along with everyone else. I stayed to watch over MaViolet, though part of me wanted to hike up and see for myself. I thought maybe if I could gaze down at that sprawling view, I'd be able to figure out a way back. After the group was out of sight, Georgie set out a line of bottled waters, a meager assortment of snacks, blinking nervously. Then he made his way out to the lot to keep watch, his rifle on its strap gently sloping across his back.

When the group returned, they funneled across the patio in a staggered line to get at the remaining waters. A wet heat radiated off Devin when he passed me, his T-shirt even blacker and clinging to him. He tossed a bottled water over Ira's head to where KJ stood, then twisted the cap from another, halving it in one pull.

Faces bronzed in sweat, Devin and the others gave their account. They could see smoke rising above what was probably our neighborhood. But they'd also seen evidence of fires elsewhere: sooty columns rising from at least three different parts of town. Was our whole neighborhood burnt, we asked, or just some of it? Could they tell which other places had been on fire? It was hard to tell beneath the haze.

All I know is we can't go back — not yet, Devin said.

Jesus, Knox said, pacing again. *It'll get better soon. It has to.*

I'd known, since the start of the unraveling, that Knox believed our problems were largely technical and logistical: the power, the weather. He knew there were sick and dangerous people, but there were more good people, he'd told me more than once. He felt sure things would start to get better as soon as they got the power back on, the planes flying again.

We need to make a sign, Knox said. *Something visible from the air.* And he did just that, later that day, along with the children. They staked out words using white plastic bags found in the café storeroom, asking me what they should write. When they finished, I walked the edge of each wavering letter: WE ARE HERE, it read.

The heat did not let up that whole afternoon. MaViolet hunched in her café chair, attempting to raise some kind of smile. I helped her get up, walked with her, arm in arm, back to the restrooms. By then, the guards had put out buckets of water; we washed our hands, ran wet paper towels over our faces.

When I was a girl, whenever Momma worked late driving buses to and from events for the high school, MaViolet would run a bath for me before supper. While I lifted clouds of bubbles in the tub, she'd finish a stew, a casserole, whatever she was cooking. Some nights Ms. Edith would stop by to leave a basket on our counter: cock-eyed cukes, wobbly green tomatoes, or some such rebellious bounty from the garden. Other nights random neighbors might drop in. If it was just the two of us eating, MaViolet let me put on one of Papa Alred's old records. Was I working hard, she wanted to know. Were those teachers of mine treating me all right? Had I found any joy that day? Now I swished soap into the bucket and helped my grandma untangle her arms from her housecoat, exposing a thin night-gown underneath. Through its pale sheerness, I could see her sturdy underthings, bright and white as bone.

You're a good girl, she said to my reflection in the mirror, but I knew she could only see certain parts of me. I bent to peel off her tall stockings, which helped with circulation, and dunked them in the filmy water. I balled up her housecoat next, figuring I'd wash her gown if we were still stranded the next day. That's when I felt the husk of something in her pocket and fished it out. It was an inhaler: *her* inhaler. I felt my guts sink. Still, I tucked it deep into my pocket, hoping MaViolet hadn't seen it along with the wave of panic that must have crossed my face. While her housecoat dried on a chair in the sun, I sat with MaViolet in the relative privacy of the theater — the door propped to allow for a wedge of light.

The afternoon sun cast orange on our limbs. Ezra started a card game with La-Toya, gambling for matches torn from stray packs. She won three times in a row then quit after Ezra kept accusing her of cheating. Devin and Elijah went back to the loop, reclaiming their chairs beyond the Jaunt. More than once, I heard Georgie's familiar refrain whenever Mr. Byrd came near: *They aren't supposed to be here, remember?* I leaned back in a café chair and tried to rest my eyes. In the blackness, I saw the boy from the pickup, his fingers spidering over a ledge. When I startled awake, Carol was not far from me, her silvery bob frazzled by the heat, her hens at her feet. She was testing Ira's forehead with the back of her hand the way you might check a child for fever. *Are we hiding,* she said. *Are we waiting?*

Ira leaned down toward the closer hen — it had reddish-brown lacing through its feathers. It pecked at Ira's hand, then skirted away. *How should I know,* Ira said.

Ms. Edith cooled herself with the fan she'd constructed from a glossy leaflet, a stubborn back-and-forth motion. *The Lord is my light, my salvation,* she said, *and whom shall I fear?*

Shuddup already, Ira told her. *Do you ever just shut the hell up?*

Hardly missing a beat, Ms. Edith flung a sharp stack of leaflets in Ira's direction, catching him in his hunched shoulder.

Ira skittered in his chair. *I can't stay here with you people!* He called out to Mr. Byrd, demanding keys to a vehicle, any vehicle.

Ms. Edith responded coolly, not looking at Ira. *If he gets keys, I get keys. I'll drive to*

Mount Zion. I'll drive to Columbia Heights.

I've got to get out of here, Ira said.

We heard a lock turn then. Our eyes all flew to the café, where Georgie had shut himself inside, separating us from most of the food and bottled water. We could see him through the glass, his features twitching with fear or excitement, his cranberry belly compressed against the glass door. Mr. Byrd was already hurrying over from the ticket office, but Ezra got to the door first. *You kidding me,* Ezra said, his back bathed in sweat. He pummeled the glass with the heel of his palm. *Oh hell no,* Ezra said.

Ezra turned as if to walk away, then doubled back, producing a handgun from the back of his shorts, pressing it flush against the glass.

Mama Yahya's arms seemed to multiply as she deftly looped in Jobari and Imani, who'd careened forward to try to get a better view. KJ's eyes were trained on Ezra too, even as the boy ferried something dark and sweet into his mouth. MaViolet pushed herself to her feet. *Young man!* she said, her face steeped in worry on top of worry. Georgie remained frozen on the other side of the glass, his eyes on Ezra's gun.

Put that away, son, Mr. Byrd was saying.

Someone must've gotten Elijah, because

he came sprinting from the Jaunt toward his twin, with Devin close behind. *C'mon now,* Elijah kept saying to Ezra, trying to peel his brother's smaller body from the door with patient hands. But Ezra bucked, threw out an elbow, knocking a grunt from Elijah's throat. Elijah cocked his arm back and struck Ezra two times on the face. In the jostling that followed, the gun fell to the ground. The twins toppled too, knocking over a tower of chairs. Elijah worked to pin Ezra down, but Ezra resisted, biting and scratching. Mr. Byrd swept the gun out of reach. Devin shouted at Ezra and Ira shouted at Elijah. Ms. Edith prayed sternly and Knox took a stumbling step back. Papa Yahya scolded his children for having been too close to danger once again. *You must listen to me,* he said.

Beside me, MaViolet winced.

I was up and teetering on my feet.

I remember looking out at all those people, most of whom I'd seen or known over months or years — several whom I loved. Everybody was yelling or cowering or sneering, angry or afraid. I blinked, and their familiar faces blurred into the profiles of the men with fire, those other faces distorted by rage. I opened my big mouth, my voice, deep like Momma's when it needed to be. I

144

remember I shouted, *We're here!*

Everybody froze. Even Ira, who'd been laughing sourly. Even Ezra, who had a bruise beginning to darken his cheek. I could feel Knox beside me, his eyes fixed on me, like he was surprised by that voice of mine. Mr. Byrd unlocked the café door, a slow turn of a key, and Georgie stood sweating in its gap. I let out a long and trembling breath.

We were together and safe, but how safe, I said. And how would we ever get home, if we couldn't work together. It was only by chance that we'd gotten away, and we were fools if we thought we were out of danger. It was up to us, just us, I said, to turn that fragile grace into something more.

Words flew from me, but afterward, they felt weightless. Above us, through the atrium, I saw a swooping silhouette: a lone bat or a sparrow in flight. It was already dusk again. A full pale moon was rising, and I felt exposed beneath it.

Weaving through a maze of chairs and people, I retreated toward the restroom. Even at the entrance, the stink of unflushed toilets hit me. I gagged but nothing came up — my body dense with a sick, held-in feeling, like I was carrying something impossibly heavy that I could not set down, not even for a moment. I leaned against the wall, flicking the switch out of habit. My fingers — even after all those weeks — still reaching for the world as it once had been.

I made my way to the sinks in the low light, feeling like I'd only added to the chaos. In the mirror, I could barely make out my reflection, my hair pulled into two messy knots, my face black and blue like the ebony sculptures Momma used to collect. I planned to come out and say to everybody, What do I know? I planned to come out and apologize.

When I finally came out, everyone was still standing near the café, their bodies close. I could hear a voice, unsteady but rising: MaViolet's voice. She was singing an old hymn I half remembered, and Ms. Edith's voice fell in too. Other folks seemed to know its rhythm, the way they swayed to it.

Thing is, MaViolet had lived on First Street most of her life and she knew everybody. Even feral kids, like KJ, who tended to come around looking hangdog near suppertime. Even the white families, like Ira and Carol, who'd begun to raze or renovate the run-down houses adjacent to First. Ms. Edith knew lots of folks too, from bringing covered dishes to the homebound, and bundles of fresh herbs and greens to everybody in Augusts past back when the community garden was bursting with color. That evening, those two old ladies sang as if our lives depended on it: MaViolet's light voice lifting up, and Ms. Edith's drum-major depth coming in underneath, so that other folks began to hum or sing, like they wanted to be held in between. When I walked toward that singing, the group pulled me in, one hand after another, until I was standing beside my grandma and part of the rough circle they'd made. I felt their gazes rising to take me in, like they wanted to hear my voice too, like it was an extension of theirs.

V.

The singing didn't save us. What saved us — what might save us yet — was the old neighborhood. Whatever else you might say about it, living on First Street schooled us in its own scraped-kneed way. Our front stoops, just big enough to hold a plastic chair or two, seemed to always hold some auntie or other hawking her head out, to make sure nobody's kid ran out into the road. To see who was about to get together. To see who was getting on whose very last nerve. Older kids keeping an eye on the younger ones, like we were all cousins. In the summers of my childhood, seemed like you could always hear the ice-cream truck down the road, its eerie carnival jingle, and the creepy pale driver who would trade hot quarters for something melty and sweet. We'd hand over our money tactically lest that man grab us and steal us away. Red tongues, sticky hands, and afterward we did a dance of survival on the sidewalk, careful not to step on the cracks, not to break our mommas' backs, which, as far as what we could tell, were already bowed toward breaking.

Along with the unraveling, First Street had transformed once again. Ms. Edith along with some ladies from her church doled out food from the garden, ragged cabbage heads and sleek eggplants, trading excess herbs with those fierce growers across Ridge. A couple of mothers distributed jugs of water from the giant cistern behind the ball courts. Some of their grown sons, along with Devin and Elijah, protected our cinderblock clubhouse, newly filled by neighbors with supplies: charcoal, canned goods, or whatever folks could get their hands on. In the evenings, in the adjacent parking lot, people bartered for cigarettes, for spirits, for Pampers. People gave away old clothing and children's toys. Early on, local churches made deliveries of cereal and soap and candles. One time a family of newer residents — a father and son with skin the color of wet sand — shot a deer in the gully behind the garden. They dressed it, shared the meat out widely before it spoiled, the charry smell rising from grills, filling our noses, all up and down First and into the greater neighborhood.

We spent that next morning at the welcome pavilion stunned and homesick, hiding or waiting — it was hard to tell which. Water bottles crinkled in our hands, the water warm and tasting of plastic. Back on First Street, and all our lives, we could reliably claim small things — *my* room, *my* sofa, *my* supper. But at the welcome pavilion, everything belonged to someone else, or to the past. Mr. Byrd had the keys, at least, and he used them, propping open doors. The kids scampered around the pavilion's outer perimeter, playing tag where the chaser carried an imaginary machine gun or a torch. MaViolet perked up, that old hymn persisting as a low hum in her throat. Devin and Elijah kept up their watch of the front entrance and woods, which separated us from the road below. They hung out and slept in the swept-out Jaunt, while Ezra, still brooding, sulked in and around the theater.

The sun was high in the sky when I saw Mama Yahya walk away. She walked with purpose, in her loose T-shirt and tight patterned wrapper of a skirt, past me and straight out of the courtyard. She left without waking Papa Yahya, who dozed in a café chair, his head falling forward as if he were nodding. She was, as always, carrying the baby, her body rocking slightly as she placed one foot in front of the other, a syncopated motion. She moved past the ticket office door, past the Jaunt, hardly turning her head. Maybe it was something in the economy of her movement, the quiet music of it, that made me follow.

At a distance, I matched Mama Yahya's pace as she continued on a paved path, bordered in wildflowers, that cut through the high tier of the parking lot. I stopped when she halted at a lone empty plot, prickling with grass. It was edged by a low split-rail fence and surrounded by parking spaces. A sign explained that historians had found the bones of slaves here, though there were no headstones or markers. At the fence line, Mama Yahya worked her lips, talking to the baby in her home language — or else the private language of mothers and children; it sounded nearly familiar.

She's probably in shock, Knox said. He'd followed me, cautiously, like I'd followed her. He was standing on the path a few paces behind me, his palms slightly lifted, as if trying not to startle me. I started to say, I'm okay. Instead I said, *That boy, in the Jeep — did you see him?*

I mean, we've all gotta be in shock — at least a little — the way those men came, Knox said.

I felt overcome by an almost unbearable lightness, like I might float up. Maybe Knox noticed too, because he wrapped his arms around me, from behind, holding me to the ground. He perched his head on top of mine, so we were looking at that unadorned burial ground together.

After a moment Knox gestured at Mama Yahya. *Let's make sure she gets safely back.*

All day, that feeling of weightlessness plagued me. Even as I tried to wash myself with a pump of soap and a bucket of rain-water. Even as I listened to MaViolet and Ms. Edith chat back and forth on a bench near the gift shop, mentally checking in on each neighbor they knew, and where they might be right then. It was only the sound of glass breaking that brought me back into my body — made fine hair along my fore-arms stand on end, as if jagged things were

151

raining down. I was up and following Mr. Byrd toward the open door of the museum, the source of that splintered sound.

Through the grayness, up a flight of stairs, we found KJ standing between the Yahya children. They weren't far from the upper doors to the museum, from which thick strands of light poured in. A hammer fell to the floor with a thud and KJ stepped back. But Jobari and Imani stood frozen before the shattered display, their eyes wide with surprise, as if they'd believed things would somehow hold. As soon as they saw us, the Yahya siblings began to wail. *Take us home!* they cried, snot percolating, tears streaking their dark, chapped cheeks.

In the broken display, a set of gadgets shone. A brass telescope on a pedestal, a pocketknife flung open with one ragged blade extended like a dragonfly's wing. I wondered, had Thomas Jefferson himself used these very tools to mark or measure. Fleeing home, we could have landed any-where, but there we were in that particular museum dedicated to my own great-great-great-grandfather. So many generations between him and me, and what did it mat-ter anymore? I reached through the newly jagged edge with wary fingers, angling toward a watch — pearl-faced and encased in a palm-sized square of wood, built to open and close like a compact mirror. Touching it, I felt a low-level currency, some sense of conduction.

What now, I thought.

Be mindful of all that sharpness, Mr. Byrd said.

The children backed away, sobbing softly, *Home.*

It was me who called everyone together, as Knox and Mr. Byrd scraped café chairs into a hasty circle. Georgie set out waters, keeping a buffer of distance from Ezra, whose jaw gleamed a deep shade of purple where his twin had struck him. Devin and Elijah came over and stood to the far right of our group, with MaViolet in a chair at a table near the middle. Before taking her place, Ms. Edith breezed through the café, picking up trail mix and dark, seeded crackers, as if she were gleaning from a garden. She set out these snacks on a table, beside the line of bottled waters. Folks snatched them up; a somber crunching commenced. At my request, Knox found and opened a package of stationery from the gift shop. Seeing it, Imani retrieved a quill pen and a pot of ink from a children's discovery room below, her face still salted in tear tracks.

Y'all wanna head back, I said, once everyone was seated and looking up toward me. *Y'all wanna see what's left, hope it's safe already? Split up? Head somewhere different? I can't say me and my grandma have anywhere else to go.*

I looked out across the open courtyard. From his bench beside Carol, Ira suffered a fit of coughing and cloaked his mouth with the crook of his arm. MaViolet gnawed at dry crackers, her body otherwise motionless. Her eyes shone, as if beams of light were radiating right from her to me. *What is it y'all wanna do?* I said.

A blistering breeze swept through, rustling stray brush. *I'm thinking we should stay here and together, for now,* I offered.

The wind died back. No one agreed aloud, but nobody disagreed either. Papa Yahya pulled his son, Jobari, closer to him. LaToya, who'd braided her hair and now sported meandering cornrows, ran her fingers over the new peaks and valleys. I tugged my frayed scooped collar up over the knob of my shoulder. *What is it we need from one another,* I said, *in this time in between?*

We sat facing one another until folks began to offer up words for what they wanted or needed. We began a short list of things we could do and would do. We agreed to talk and listen. We promised we would try not to fight with each other. Knox wrote each thing down on the parchment-colored stationery, in his left-handed script, careful not to smear the ink. The hens squawked, as if in agreement, and everybody laughed.

Then Ezra called out, *We oughta fry those birds up good!* And I couldn't help but think of Brown's corner store, the boxes of battered wings Devin and I had shared. My mouth filled with water. How hungry I felt for the past.

Don't be foolish, boy, Ms. Edith said. *You'd trade one meal of meat for an egg or two every day?*

From her chair beside Ira's, Carol mouthed, Thank you.

They drank their wine, Elijah persisted. *They drank without offering anything to anybody. No disrespect, Ms. Edith, but what makes you think they about to share even one little egg with us?*

Ira grasped the edge of the chair he sat in. *It was mine!* he said. *I had every right!* But then he looked out into the fan of leaves in the courtyard, as if they were flames. *They always come, don't they, sooner or later? Well armed, right? Fueled by lies! Carrying those disgraceful flags.* When Ira spoke of flags, I remembered how the men on First Street had all worn blue armbands, though I hadn't been able to see the emblem clearly. *I guess I hoped I might not live to see it,* Ira said.

We'll share our eggs! Carol said, rubbing Ira's back, which now convulsed beneath her hand. *We will,* she said.

We pressed on, fleshing out our makeshift treaty. We talked each proposition up and down, or sometimes just nodded assent. We agreed to collect and share all the food and drink we found on the mountain. We agreed to borrow and use any supplies or tools we needed, from the shops and staff areas and even the displays. Georgie tipped his chin up but continued to move from table to table, carrying our trash away.

The things on the mountain, along with what little we'd brought, made a strange assortment. We had basic first aid supplies and a large collection of tools. We had chips, granola bars, crackers, pretty tins of tea. We had bags of old-timey dark chocolate drops covered in white sprinkles, which MaViolet said reminded her of ones she'd eaten when she was a girl. We had the shaky promise of eggs, and many, many tins of Virginia peanuts glistening beneath silvery vacuum seals. Earlier, I'd seen Ms. Edith squinting at a display of heirloom seeds in the garden section of the gift shop. Now she was schooling us on how to keep the hens properly grazed, and on some of the things that grew free in Virginia that we might eat — things she'd eaten around her mother's garden as a child. *Ditch lilies, dandelions, morels, chickweed.* The way she said it sounded like she was quoting Scripture.

You were born in Virginia? I asked Ms. Edith. She looked at me hard, her brow furrowed like she might just send me off to fetch my own whupping switch from some tree. But then she answered, locating her beginnings in widening circles: She was born in her Granny Lee's house at the end of what the colored folks called Harp Street, near Shadwell, in the Piedmont, in North America, on God's green earth.

Papa Yahya said, after fleeing violence in the Republic of Congo, he'd waited for years in a camp in Tanzania, surviving on almost nothing, not even enough clean drinking water; he'd waited so long, he'd begun to wonder which was better: to be brutalized all at once or to die slowly of attrition, of thirst? Mr. Byrd said that there were large collection pools for rain, designed by Jefferson himself, water that could be drawn up by pumps. *Up at the house,* he said, and I felt a throbbing at my temples. I did not think we should go back to town — not yet — but I did not want to go into that museum of a house on the hill either. I imagined we would stay at the welcome pavilion, for a few days, then something would happen, a signal to tell us what to do.

We all agreed we would protect one another. Knox wrote that down too.

No matter what, Devin called out.

No matter what, we echoed.

No matter what, we promised.

We decided that, for now, Mr. Byrd and I would hold keys. And Ms. Edith, along with Carol, would portion out a quantity of food for everybody, morning and evening. We would take turns and help as we were able. We'd keep working all together until we could go home again.

After we talked, Devin and Elijah, along with Mr. Byrd, parked Mr. Byrd's Town Car below the broken gate, backed into woods and covered with brush, then blocked the entrance road above it using one of Monticello's gas-strapped shuttles. We took this precaution even as we told ourselves that the armed men would not come out this far. They only wanted town, we said, recalling the way they'd stopped chasing us at

the edge of it. We nearly convinced ourselves.

We all agreed we would use what we
needed, but we would not destroy anything
at Monticello for the sake of bitterness at
all we'd lost and seemed to still be losing.
Knox penned this in too, another article in
our hasty constitution. In our words and
shared intentions, things seemed to shift
slightly between us. Ira bid good night to
Ms. Edith in a gruff but crumbling voice,
and Ms. Edith waved him off, but less
harshly than before, briefly lifting her
fingers from her new assortment of slick
seed packs. Papa Yahya paraded his children,
along with KJ, into the gift shop. He
prompted each child to choose something
special to take and hold — a large golden
commemorative coin, a wooden toy cipher
for coding and decoding, a soft plush
animal that recalled a real one that had once
roamed fierce and free in Virginia. Papa
Yahya held fresh gift-shop T-shirts up to
each child's pigeon-chest, judging the width
of their shoulders. And I could not help but
think of Momma, how she used to heap
what little she had onto my back when I
was their age. Bright clothes, decent shoes,
my hair always done, my parts like little
prayers, as if to say, as she sent me out into

the world, Take care of this child, this child is loved.

Papa Yahya collected an armful of books from the children's reading section, all of them about Thomas Jefferson's long, remarkable life. *They should know this man,* I heard him say. *A great and good man.*

We woke to a change in weather. We woke to baleful winds whipping over our bodies, the open sky above Knox and me churning to a muddy gray. The winds knocked creaks from treetops and flattened blades of grass inches from my face. Propped up in her padded set of chairs, MaViolet opened her eyes. As I made my way to her, stray hairs levitated around her chamomile-colored face. She struggled to straighten one knee, then the other. Dropping pressure always flared up her arthritis. "Arthur," she called it. I leaned in close.

You all right, MaVi?

Got to be, she said as I worked my arms around her to help her to stand.

I thought I would say something useful. I meant to say, Let's get you inside, indicating the café or the museum. Instead, a long gust ballooned the fresh gift-shop T-shirt I wore and filled MaViolet's housecoat so that it flared like a sail behind her.

160

It's time we go up to the house, I said.

Could be past time, Grandbaby.

I knew it then: We would go up. We were going.

Near the café patio, Carol was portioning out granola bars and chocolate and nuts. Ms. Edith directed Ezra to bring out a new crate of waters. Folks murmured about the wind as they chewed and peered out from under the eaves. Those earlier storms had made us all deeply suspicious of weather.

The house, I said, moving from one table to the next: *I think we might need to go up to get out of the storm.* Ira brushed crumbs from his mouth, and Mama Yahya smiled into the face of her cooing baby. Papa Yahya reshaped my query into a singsong declaration: *We will go up to the house!* Jobari and Imani sang it back to him. *To the house!*

Mr. Byrd peered up between the trees, his hair lifted in the wind like a bright storm cloud. When he told Georgie what we planned to do, the younger man began to rock. *But Mrs. Dandridge said,* Georgie began. This time, Mr. Byrd responded loud enough for all of us nearby to hear. *Listen, Georgie,* he said, *I don't give a rat's ass what Mrs. Dandridge told us. Mrs. Dandridge drove off with her big-headed dogs, remember? We're the ones still here.*

We're supposed to protect the house, Georgie answered, his tone pleading, but Mr. Byrd clasped Georgie's slumping shoulders. *Didn't you hear what happened to these people? Don't forget, Mrs. Dandridge handed me the keys. You're a good man, George, but maybe the time has come that I release you —*

Georgie's chin dipped and I couldn't quite hear the first thing he said. But I saw how his chest crumpled and his words, whatever they were, sounded choked. His reaction made me imagine that, apart from Monticello, Georgie led a solitary life. A cabin on the edge of someone else's property, maybe. I felt for him — I wanted to tell him I knew something about loss.

I — I can stay, Georgie said, brushing away tears. *I can help!*

For a moment, the wind died back, sounding like the inside of a shell.

Knox was helping Ms. Edith with the food when I walked over, squeezed his shoulder. I'd be right back, I told him.

On my own, I made my way to the Jaunt, still parked crookedly along the loop. I hadn't set foot inside since we'd fled. *Hello,* I called into the open door, compelling my legs up the stairs, hardly tipping my body in. *Hey!*

The driver's seat had a small tear in it.

162

The inside of the bus smelled like rain and the bodies of years of commuters, maybe of our bodies too. My eyes flitted along the broken back windows, but I didn't see anybody. I might've retreated, but my feet on the top step made some kind of sound.

Devin sat up from a bucket seat in one smooth gesture, dark hair wreathing his head.

Elijah jumped up from a couple seats back, on the opposite side. His massive feet, clad in high-tops, had been planted in the aisle. He rubbed sleep from his eyes.

I'll wait out here, I said.

When Devin came down the steps a moment later, he scanned the entrance, the lot. *Everything cool?* he said. He took in my weary nod without meeting my eyes, surveying the new storminess of the morning. He had on a fresh T-shirt; he laced his arms across his chest. Elijah jumped down from the back door and walked out of view. Devin leaned his back against the Jaunt, and I wanted to say something true to him.

Thank you, I said, *for real, for what y'all did, for everybody. On First Street, I mean.*

Elijah came back, hit Devin up for a smoke.

You think this'll be bad as those others? Elijah said, looking above the trees. Of

163

course there was no way to know. I told them there was talk of going up to the house. I put it on the older folks, and on the children. They shouldn't be out in weather like that.

Devin kept looking everywhere but at me. I dared a glimpse of his face, a small plunder. *Y'all should come too,* I said.

Elijah chuckled and Devin palmed his Zippo. I rocked on my dirty sneakers, readying my feet to leave. *Anyhow, we're going up,* I told them.

Mr. Byrd led us, angling another branch turned walking stick out before him, one knobby end pressing against the pathway. That path, broad and tree-lined, promised to deliver us to Thomas Jefferson's plantation home, self-designed, well over two hundred years old, and largely built by his slaves. We'd set out from the museum end of the patio, topping a flight of steps where a life-size statue of Jefferson stood on a landing, glinting in metal, not far from where I used to check tourists' bags. Our footfalls against the pale pebbles made a shushing sound.

Stray raindrops began to pelt our heads, but the leaves above us took the brunt of the first waves of rainfall. Mr. Byrd had traded his cranberry polo for a novelty T-shirt from the gift shop, made to mimic the scrawl of the Declaration of Independence. As he moved ahead of our group, Thomas Jefferson's words undulated across his back: *We hold these truths to be self-evident, that all men are created equal.*

We carried a jumble of supplies. Ms. Edith had laced her arms with tote bags filled with food, and seeds, and tea. Carol and Ira carried one hen each along with Ira's now bulging leather satchel. Ezra hefted a case of bottled waters, and KJ shadowed him, pulling his pea-green suitcase through the pebbles as if he imagined wheels. Knox carried his messenger bag, newly fattened with supplies. He helped me to support MaViolet, with him on one side and me on the other as we facilitated her slow shuffle. Above her tall stockings, I could see the bright naked caps of her knees with each step. Her senior year, she'd been lead majorette, marching across the field in high white boots and a uniform marked by golden epaulets. Back then, she could throw the baton high and always catch it, a result of relentless practice, she'd told me. Now she stumbled up that path, full of effort. It was steeper than I remembered, with gullies carved along the edge to capture runoff.

Her house slippers kept filling with tiny rocks. Periodically, I helped her to empty them.

There had been, according to Mr. Byrd, at least one remaining shuttle cart down in the lot that we might have used to drive her up. But the batteries had been run down to nothing, with Mrs. Dandridge zipping herself around the property, directing the remaining workers to keep everything ready, to keep the generators running, as if this shining performance of normalcy would bring the world back.

From one section of the path we could see that empty stretch of road below where we'd driven the Jaunt in a few days earlier. We were already hustling to beat the full onset of rain, but when we saw the road and the hastily blocked entrance, we all picked up our pace. LaToya high-stepped in her foamy flip-flops. Ms. Edith huffed mightily, naming growing things between harsh breaths. Ira pushed his hand off a tree dividing the path, asking how much farther we had. I drew MaViolet forward too, so quickly that Knox asked me to slow down, just a little.

The storm, I said to explain my haste, calling on that more immediate anxiety. I was wishing Devin and Elijah had walked up

166

with us, but they'd remained down at the welcome pavilion, "to keep watch," along with Georgie, resurrecting an old set of walkies the guards had been using before we'd arrived.

Up ahead I could see a bend in the path, then a short set of stairs that led up to the Jefferson cemetery. When I'd worked at Monticello, shuttle buses would pause below the family cemetery so that tourists could gaze at Thomas Jefferson's obelisk gravestone. The walking path passed the cemetery too, with its black metal fencing, the gravel shifting to a tight brick mosaic beneath our footfalls. Our group paused at the locked gate, where a black-and-gold sign welcomed Jefferson's descendants and warded off strangers. Through the spire-topped pickets, we eyed rows of stone markers, many of them engraved with the Randolph family name. Briskly, we set off walking again, the path splitting a high pasture between a feeble allée of wispy trees. *MaVi, we're almost there,* I said.

Up out of the woods, the storm felt closer. The wind reared up, hounding our backs. We kept our eyes low even as, to our right, we spied the wooden trellises that marked the head of the sprawling vegetable garden. Straight ahead, the first of several spotty monuments to slavery exposed themselves. The burnt-out ruins of a chimney. A reconstructed cabin made of roughly hewn wood. A bare plot of ground marked by the lowliest sign, with not even the remnants of a building: DWELLING FOR ENSLAVED PEOPLE. Sloped down to our right, we could see the full layout of the garden, rows of growing things with reddish-brown pathways in between like the parts in LaToya's hair. Mr. Byrd told us that the unpaved stretch we were moving along was called Mulberry Row. I remembered the name as he said it: Certain slaves would have worked here, forging nails, weaving fabric.

Everything at the top of that hill felt new to me that morning, transfigured from the times I'd come before, for school trips, for work. Before, there'd always been some measure of distance, a wall between whatever Monticello was and my real life. Real life was Momma, MaViolet, my friends. Real life was school and my determination to do something that mattered. To do something for other people, especially people like the ones I'd grown up with, who were all too often undermined and undervalued. I'd kept real life in one place, and the imagined life of my ancestors in another unexamined place, like a room with no windows. Now my real life flailed and smoked behind me. Now *this* was my life. Walking up, I felt myself seesawing again between density and lightness, between Momma's disavowal of this painful heritage and MaViolet's cautious regard.

The rain blew in, pummeled our skin. We hunched in anticipation. The children ran ahead. Up the steps to our left, we could see the long L-shaped walkway of the southern terrace, with little rooms turned exhibits tucked beneath its bent arm. Above it, the grand white dome of the main house rose, like Monticello on the nickels I used to stack on my dresser as a child. Mr. Byrd led us up toward the eastern entrance: the way we would've come, in carriages or shuttles, had we been sanctioned guests.

We hustled toward the east porch, trying to beat the full force of the coming rain. Still I managed to take in that view of the house, its handsome brick and double-storied windows framed by green shutters. The foursome of sand-colored columns, which lifted a bright white triangle — the pediment — above the porch. The weather-vane on the roof looked askew, but otherwise the building looked just the same, as if nothing had changed, or ever would. I couldn't help but imagine black hands too, sunk in mortar. *My Monticello.* The words formed low and unbidden in my throat, barely parting my lips to escape.

VI.

We scrambled up stone steps, pausing beneath the east porch to recover our breath. From that entrance, all the unsavory evidence of slavery was hidden down the slope we'd just dragged ourselves up. The front yard looked feral, tall weeds rising from nappy grass. I imagined eight-year-old Momma waiting by the shuttle stop, beyond the linden trees.

Let's go in, folks were saying.

I leaned against the nearest column, legs trembling, feeling hesitant again now that we'd arrived. That was when I heard a hollow rasping beneath the howl of wind. The sound was coming from MaViolet. Her face had gone rigid. She gripped my arm so tightly, I felt my own chest seize.

Together Knox and I shuttled her to the wooden bench built at the porch's edge, ignoring the slant spray of rain. Everybody huddled around her, watching as she tried and failed to take in air.

What's the matter with her? Imani said, tugging her mother's skirt.

Help her already! Ira said.

Ms. Edith pressed her palms together. *Lord have mercy.*

MaViolet used to have these breathless attacks when I was younger, and they'd crept back in the last handful of years. But before the unraveling, we could call her doctor or 911. With her free hand, MaViolet clutched at herself, like she was trying to cradle her own body. All I could think to do in my panic was drop to my knees at her feet. Holding her gaze, I drew in my own breath, with deliberation, as if I could lavish my breath on her or coax her air to flow like mine. Then, fumbling, I remembered and dug in my pocket, producing that thing she could not find in hers. I uncapped her inhaler with jittery hands, shook it, and brought it to her parted lips.

For you are my fortress, my refuge in times of trouble, Ms. Edith said.

As MaViolet nursed the inhaler, I freed myself from her grasp. I rose enough to pull the messenger bag from Knox's body, though I knew the answer already. Nonetheless, I paddled through his things like they were mine too, as if I had, in fact, grabbed what I now understood I most needed: that plastic bag the nurse had handed me guiltily at MaViolet's last doctor's visit. But of course, it was not there.

171

From my place at her feet, I looked up at my grandma's honeyed face. Slowly, the color was coming back into her cheeks. *We're at the house,* I said.

The rain fell loose and hard around us.

Watch your step, Mr. Byrd said. *Let's get her inside.*

Walking into Monticello that first day felt like breaking a seal, our breath greeting hot, stagnant air. We moved into the entrance hall, a room faced in windows, MaViolet's body light against mine.

Right away, I displaced a barrier near the door — a waist-high wooden stand connecting an arm's length of rope — meant to cordon off that front corner. Some of the chairs had ribbon pulled tautly across them, blocking them from use. I asked Mr. Byrd for something sharp from his tool belt and used it to slash one ribbon, then another. MaViolet sat in the first freshly liberated chair.

Grandbaby, she said.

MaVi, I said, *I'm right here —*

She let her head loll back, closing her eyes. I could hear her breathing continue to ease, like it always had before, and my panic easing with it. Her chest, exposed at the scoop of her housecoat, rose and fell, her face filling with a newly euphoric glow. *You're go-*

ing to be all right! I said, hugging her.

That entrance hall held so many things; in that moment, it held us too. High up to my right, a set of dark trophies marked the wall, mounted antlers of elk and moose. On the opposite wall, a plunder of artifacts from Native peoples: an ax, a quiver, moccasins that must have once held feet, a radial shield centered by feathers — Lakota Sioux, Mr. Byrd later told me. There were white marble busts, and the draped curves of a sculpted woman. There was a massive mastodon jaw bronzed with age. One object right up against another, curated, it seemed, by someone with broad aspirations and enormous self-regard.

Papa Yahya doubled back to the door to step out of his shoes. *Kweli, kweli,* he said softly, leaving them neatly by the entrance, proceeding in dark dress socks and looking oddly dignified, despite the cargo shorts he wore. Mama Yahya hastened her children to remove their shoes too, and KJ copied them. Mr. Byrd stood on the threshold, looking through those large glass doors at the storm.

MaViolet touched the bone of my hip, a small push in.

When I'd taken tours of Monticello in the past, I'd kept my head down, kept my hands to myself. This time, I ran fingers along the

173

top of MaViolet's chair; the painted wood felt slightly oily to the touch. I crossed the room to test the bottom rung of a ladder that stretched up toward a series of weights, attached to Jefferson's great clock above the main entrance. That whole contraption suggested an effortful passing of time — the necessity of someone to wind it. When the clock was wound, a cord strung with cannonball weights would slowly descend along one wall, revealing the days of the week, which were written at intervals from the ceiling to a hole in a floor. I peered down into the depression: It looked to have been Saturday for some time.

That morning, gazing up at Monticello's grand clock, I began an accounting of days, not only what happened within each, but also their unfurling number.

Mr. Byrd closed the front door as our tight group began to unknot itself. Lost-looking without his twin, Ezra set off through the parlor's double doors, designed by Jefferson himself to part in tandem. Ira and Carol hurried off to the left side of the house while the Yahyas, along with KJ, wandered in the opposite direction, the children murmuring excitedly. Still in her loose gold T-shirt, La-Toya followed Ms. Edith and Mr. Byrd. Finally, only Knox remained at my side, with MaViolet resting in the chair behind us. I crossed the room to where a map of Africa hung. Wordlessly, Knox joined me so that we stood shoulder to shoulder in front of it. Its proportions looked accurate enough — teal topography etched all along the coastline — but the continent's center had been left falsely empty. I moved to the map of Virginia, a few feet away, borderless and drawn full of careful lines. Nearby, a painted portrait of Thomas Jefferson himself caught my eye, glimmering in a gilded frame. I pushed up to my tiptoes to better examine his face: his ruddy cheeks and gray hair tinged with amber. Behind us wind or water battered panes of glass.

Isn't it strange, Knox said at my back, *for us — for you — to be here?*

Knox already knew about my tricky lineage. I'd told him just after he came home from spring recess, after he'd visited his family and before the grid went down. We'd been lying in bed in his small tidy dorm room, my hand on his chest, which felt smoother than I remembered from a week earlier. He was making his own confession to me, his hands plunged into my hair. My whole body had ached with a guilty kind of want, the desire to put space between our relationship and the thing I'd done with

Devin in Knox's absence. *I think my father hates me,* Knox had said, burying his head at my throat. His fan whirred in the window above us; we could never have imagined that the power would go out so soon. *He wouldn't even look at me,* Knox said, and in my desperation to comfort him, I let my own truth slip out: *Did you know my middle name is Hemings,* I'd told him. *Do you know who Sally Hemings was?*

Knox had raised his face to examine mine. *I do, actually.*

That day, Knox accepted my announcement calmly, as if I'd recited a natural number, something clear and bounded. The detached way he'd responded had made me feel almost safe that I'd shared it with him. *That's kind of cool,* he'd said.

I regained my footing below Jefferson's portrait before I answered Knox. *It's crazy to be here,* I said.

In my mind, I ran back through the parchment rules we'd written at the welcome pavilion. We would not hurt anything for the sake of hurting it, but we were *not* tourists. I slashed each ribbon and blocking rope in that first room, feeling a mixture of relief and indignation. We were out of the storm, MaViolet was breathing — but these rooms had been kept so pristine, while our homes in town had been treated like kindling. Upstairs, I could hear the call-and-response slap of KJ's bare feet between the thumping slide of the Yahya children's socked ones. All at once, they appeared on the landing, along a banister draped in pelts, with Papa Yahya calling after them.

Our group ventured into nearly every room that first day. We moved up narrow stairwells into the thickening heat, then back down again. In Jefferson's day, those stairwells had been used by slaves as well as celebrated guests, eyes averted, I imagined, one group always yielding. We rounded the perimeter of the giant dome room, with its vaulted cap of white above us, its large circular windows like a row of eyes. From up there, the sky felt so close, as if it were only a larger dome made of wind and cloud and water. I thought of Devin then: Was he out of the storm and safe down below us? Would he abandon us for town, or elsewhere? Did he hate me now?

On the second floor, we moved in and out of more bedrooms, each space dominated by some particular color or pattern, containing some version of a high bed, occasionally canopied in cloth. We found several bedrolls and a pile of sheets stacked in a mocking arrangement of domesticity, which we later divvied up and used in earnest. We stumbled into a low-ceilinged nursery that held a trundle bed, a crib, a set of porcelain-faced dolls — the children would soon sleep there, with Mama and Papa Yahya claiming the room beside it. These rooms had been carefully decorated with everyday objects — a teacup, a hairbrush, a long blue robe, a pair of woolen slippers — like set pieces for a play.

Back on the ground level, we explored the parlor, the dining room, another bedroom with a hearth. Finally we made our way through Jefferson's own rambling suite: his personal library and cabinet room, crowded with dusty books and shiny gadgets. The floor space in the cabinet was so broken up by desks and seating, it was hard to move freely. The walls were partitioned by large windows, which Jefferson must've looked out of, at all he thought he owned. Knox and I brought MaViolet through those rooms.

We came in here that other time, she said.

When they brought you for that reunion, MaVi?

MaViolet touched the high edge of a red chair. *They took us on a tour.*

After her formal visit to Monticello, they'd

asked MaViolet if she might be willing to attend an event or two in town, part of an upcoming series. I escorted her once, back in the fall, to a talk at the public library. I'd watched from the front row as she sat in church clothes at the edge of a panel of other descendants of Monticello's slaves. That particular event was centered around an auction the Jefferson family had held in 1827 at Thomas Jefferson's behest, to try to preserve the estate after his passing. Among other things, more than one hundred Black people were sold to pay off the debt Jefferson had incurred during his long and comfortable life, and to preserve the land for his white offspring. One Black descendant on the panel, who wore cufflinks and a vest, had spent many years researching his family history. He counseled us: When contacting a white person to whom you might be related by blood and or bondage, don't tell them you're Black, not until the very end of the phone call. *When you tell them you're Black,* he cautioned, *nine times out of ten, their earlier curiosity about family will dry up. More often than not, they'll hang up on you,* he said. *Sometimes, right before they hang up, they'll ask, What do you want from me?*

This man talked about one of his ancestors, a freed former slave who'd attended

Jefferson's auction to try to emancipate family members. Except there was no way to afford them all. So whom to purchase, wife or son, and whom to watch be sold off to cotton and oblivion and worse? Listening, I'd tried not to imagine how it might have felt to choose between buying Momma or MaViolet. To be on the auction block myself, facing the loss of everything I knew and everyone I loved.

It was springtime when I came before, MaViolet said. *There were tulips.*

We escorted MaViolet into Thomas Jefferson's own bedchamber, with Mr. Byrd walking close behind us. Tall blue walls and a nightstand and a high alcove bed. The bed sat between the bedroom proper and the cabinet room. Boxed in at head and toe, that singular bed spilled open into both rooms, with curtains and a stand that could be used to partition either side. Mr. Byrd told us it had been redesigned for Thomas Jefferson after his wife Martha's death. Mr. Byrd drew the curtain all the way back.

Knox and I shuffled MaViolet toward that bed, already made up with stiff white sheets. A quartet of pillows occupied the head, balanced by a comforter folded at the foot.

Lie down, MaVi, I said. It came out like a question, like I was asking somebody's permission.

MaViolet turned her body, eyeing that room — the brass-framed mirrors and the small painting of a naked white woman and a cherub. The skylight high above her that looked like an ordinary window, except for its odd placement in the ceiling. The pristine bedpan at her feet. She touched the bedsheet, hastening to bring up a knee, to give that bed her weight. We helped her to arrange herself, using the pillows to prop her up, her back against one wall, so that she might breathe more easily. On the wall at her feet, an obelisk clock hung, framed by two ancient-looking pistols and a sword.

I could sleep for days, she said.

After MaViolet was resting comfortably, we resumed our exploration. Soon we were calling out to everybody, following each other down to the final floor below. The stairwell was so steep and tight, a sign midway warned tourists: WATCH YOUR HEAD. Downstairs the air felt cooler and dank. It was dim enough that we had to go slowly to let our eyes adjust.

In the basement, there was an all-weather pass, which had granted slaves hidden access to the house, Mr. Byrd explained. There were cellars and a large cylinder of an icehouse. Off to one far end there were modern restrooms for tourists, and an old-time privy — where we would soon set up a mirror, squares of cloth, and a bucket of water, for our use.

We milled through the central basement exhibit populated by life-size cutouts of some of the known slaves of Monticello — the named cooks and butlers and nannies who'd served the Jefferson family indoors and intimately. Near there, Mr. Byrd handed out a couple of flashlights and led us into a back-of-the-house space, an informal second library full of reference books. This room sat out of time, ringed in mismatched seating as if furnished from thrift-store finds. It felt more like the rooms we'd left behind in town. We funneled in, most of us finding seats.

Mr. Byrd spoke into his walkie. A beat of static, then I could hear Devin's measured voice answer: All was quiet below.

I let the beam of my flashlight rove the chairs and books; by chance, it landed on a poster-sized photograph on the far wall, cheaply framed and hanging crookedly. Toward the middle of the image, I swear I saw an echo of my own face, lighter and wider but so familiar, as if I'd been projected into the future. I looked again and it was, for real, MaViolet's face. In the picture, she stood in better health, on the west porch stairs, beneath Monticello's dome. She was squeezed in a tiered row, along with a good number of other Black folks and a few fairer-skinned ones. In the image, MaViolet wore a pillbox hat, crowned with pale purple feathers. They must've taken that picture when they brought her here last spring.

Ms. Edith was standing near the door. *That our Violet?* she said.

Carol stroked the hen in her lap as if it were a cat. *It does look something like her.*

Mr. Byrd explained that the photo showed some of the known Black families of Monticello. Descendants of the more than six hundred slaves Jefferson had owned over his lifetime, most of whom had lived somewhere on this plantation, a few near the house, the majority in the vast acreage below. Among this group were a few of Thomas Jefferson's own Black great-great-great-grandchildren, fathered with my namesake, a young slave he also owned. When Mr. Byrd said this, I felt everybody's eyes on me, outed as I was by that grainy picture. Now they squinted in the dimness as if my shadowy features might provide clarity. Mr. Byrd dipped his chin like he was asking which group MaViolet and I belonged to. *Sally Hemings,* I said softly, turning her name over in my mouth. *My middle name is Hemings.* I told them, like I'd told Knox, who was holding one of my hands so hard it felt like he was squeezing the blood from my fingers. My stomach hurt, still I kept talking: *My whole name is Da'Naisha Hemings Love.*

Had Momma gifted me that middle name grudgingly or defiantly? What am I supposed to do with these ancestors, I wondered, and what would these neighbors make of me and MaViolet now that they knew? Would they see us as more worthy, or less worthy, as the descendants of a founding father and a slave? And what did it even matter now?

I looked at MaViolet's small bright face in the picture.

We are descendants, I said.

When I said this, Ezra was like, *Damn,* and Carol, for some reason, broke out in a slow clap. I must've shot her some kind of look because she stopped at once, her hands still pressed together. Papa Yahya moved closer to inspect the picture, sucking his teeth. *But how do you know?* he said.

There were oral histories, corroborating facts, rumors, and published accounts going all the way back to Jefferson's own time. There had been a commission and a counter-commission, along with DNA analysis connecting Jefferson's known descendants to one of Sally Hemings's known descendants. But mostly I knew my lineage the way most families know theirs: I knew because Momma told me, because MaViolet told her.

Someone from Monticello called my grandma, I told them.

I thought Papa Yahya might question me further or scrunch up his face like I imagined Momma's third-grade teacher had. Instead he nodded obligingly, like he was impressed. As if, on the word of someone from Monticello's staff, he could accept my claim as legitimate.

I might have said more, but Jobari and Imani both jumped up, their limbs flinging out with excitement. *Are our pictures here too, somewhere in this house? We shall go and find them!* Ira pushed up from his recliner, lifting a fat bird in his arms. Rosegold LaToya uncrossed her pale limbs. *So y'all are like hood royalty or something,* she said.

Knox kept hold of my hand, and I wanted it back, just for a moment.

We are descendants, I said once more.

I tried to keep my head up.

I decided to keep my head up.

Damn, Ezra said again.

The wind wore itself out quickly, scattering brush and fallen branches across the yard before dying down. But the rain kept on, wavering between downpours and jumpy showers. It must've been afternoon when I wandered out on the southern terrace, a planked boardwalk, with one bend in it, that extended toward Mulberry Row. From there I could see Ms. Edith, under a heavy mist. She was tromping along the ridge above the garden, surveying the once-tidy rows. She'd found rain boots and now wore them, along with a clear plastic leaf bag fashioned into a poncho. With translucence billowing around her thin frame, she shouted across the distance to me and to Mama Yahya, who stood behind me under the eaves. Arms thrust into a giant Y, Ms. Edith announced that there were stray stands of chard in the garden, peas climbing, a hedge of blackberries. All of it half ravaged by heat or rain or rabbits or birds, but still. Cheering, the children followed her down the hill to accost the bramble, filling their mouths with purple. Later we would find hand tools and dig for radishes, yams.

When I turned to walk back in, Mama

Yahya was gone, and there was Knox, looking right at me. I realized I'd avoided being completely alone with him since we'd gone inside the house. Now everybody had separated again, and he stood by himself at a large open window, which rose from the floor to make a doorway. He lifted the glass higher. I made my way to him, ducking to enter.

Are you okay, Da'Naisha? he said.

Inside it was too warm, the small room dominated by windows. There was slate flooring, a desk, a chair. A few ceramic pots held dwarf lemon trees, their desiccated bodies bowed and leafless.

I'm fine, I said, but I might've said, *I'm breathing. I'm still alive and trying.*

I was thinking, Knox said, *we could sleep in this room.* He reached out as if to touch my elbow but then withdrew his hand and proceeded with his voice instead. *There's plenty of light, and it's near your grandmother, but private —*

I felt unsteady, like I needed to lie down, but there was no bed, so I held myself upright. I tugged at the ragged hem of my shorts, all those loose fat threads. *I feel like something bad is gonna happen. Because of me. Because I brought us here,* I said.

Knox surveyed the small room. *It's fine to*

187

be here. We had to go someplace, he said. I
guess he saw this was not helping me,
because he tried again, coming in from a
different angle. *My father says our family is
related to Arthur Armstrong Denny — part of
that group of settlers who founded Washington
State — we all have ancestors, I mean.*

It's not the same, I said.

I know, he said, then more softly, *I know,*
like he got it. *But you are, like, related to
him, right?*

I'm related to her, I told him. When I said
this, I wondered, had she ever felt safe here?
I'm named after her.

Knox lowered himself to the floor by the
open window, folding his lanky body so that
he looked much smaller. *They had children
together,* he said. *Do you think he cared about
her? Do you think it's possible she loved him
at all?*

I wanted him to stop talking. I wanted to
walk deep out into the muddy yard. *How
are you supposed to love somebody,* I said,
who has that much power over you?

I know, Knox said. *The whole situation is
so . . . wrong, so . . . outrageous. All I'm trying
to say is, even in small ways, doesn't one
person always have more power than another?* Knox said this like he was asking me

188

something personal, like he was asking, *Is it possible for you to love me?*

I felt so shaky then, but I kept standing. I was thinking, what did it mean if I loved Knox: Did it mean I hated something in myself? Or was the dark feeling in my gut something older, something outside of me and him?

I shouldn't have brought us here, I said. *Maybe we should try to go somewhere else.*

The Jaunt, Knox said. *I wouldn't trust it to get us far. Also, your grandmother . . .*

Still, I said.

Everything about that room, the whole house, felt like it was swaying. I sat down on the slate floor across the door from Knox, holding my knees, trying to steady myself. Knox seemed to have abandoned that intimate line of questions and turned his attention to more practical ones. *Don't worry, we'll figure it out,* he said, reaching for me, his hand bright against my skin. He tugged me toward him, and I crawled the short rest of the way, my knees scraping stone. We sat in the window, his larger body wrapped around mine, rocking a little. The acrid smell of sweat and rain, his chin resting easily on my head. *I'm just saying,* Knox went on, *it's crazy, it's . . . incredible: This house is like partway yours.*

■ ■ ■ ■

That night and the next morning, our group met in the red-chaired parlor and the west porch that spilled from it. We met to fill our stomachs with warm things: a porridge mix Ms. Edith found in the upper gift shop, blended with boiling water. We sprinkled it with sea salt and peas for supper, Ezra and KJ wrinkling their noses. We laced it with maple syrup for breakfast — Jobari and Imani cheered. We met to work out a rotating schedule of who would cook or clean or tend the garden. We came together to sing and to check in on one another, signaled by Mr. Byrd or Ms. Edith ringing a bell.

Before our first supper, we gathered fallen wood; we pulled it out of the weather and stacked it beneath the reliable dryness of the all-weather pass. We inspected our wavery reflections in the rain-rippled surface of water pumped up from one of Jefferson's cisterns. We tested the water on our tongues, and when it tasted flat, Mama Yahya showed us how to pour it back and forth between two vessels, to infuse it with air again.

Each person claimed a space to sleep that first day. Ms. Edith laid her book of psalms on a chair in an octagonal room on the first floor. She shared out the display of sheets, saving one set to shroud her own high alcove bed. Mr. Byrd quietly housed his tools in the square bedroom between Ms. Edith's and the entrance hall. Even though it was cooler on the ground level, other folks went up, opening windows in this house that kept reminding us it was designed for a time before air-conditioning or electric light. La-Toya disappeared into a second-floor room patterned in blue and white, hardly emerging except sometimes for food. Ezra claimed a bedroom on the third floor, with protruding skylight windows and two beds along one wall. Carol and Ira carried furnishings out to the white textile workshop, a free-standing building on Mulberry Row, so that they could more comfortably stay there. Mr. Byrd helped them cordon off an outdoor space near that building, to house and shelter their precious hens.

After our first supper, I petitioned that MaViolet should remain in Thomas Jefferson's own bedchamber. *Is that right,* Papa Yahya said, but then his attention orbited back to the children who were fighting over a wooden horse they'd found. Ira made a face as if to protest, but then swallowed his complaint along with his last lumpy spoonful. Ms. Edith said, *I don't see why not.* So with the clang of silverware, it was decided: MaViolet would stay perched in Jefferson's boxed-in bed. Folks dropped in to see her, with Ms. Edith getting Knox to bring in a comfortable chair for her longer visitations. Most people came in pairs, because of Ma-Violet's new reserve. She'd greet them, of course, offer a trembling smile. But after an exchange of pleasantries, her thoughts seemed to drift off, or else she'd close her eyes. Her guests would be left to talk among themselves, saying they knew she'd be up again soon before slipping out. Fleeing the men, the hike up the hill — all of it had cost her something. Even so, when I went and sat beside her, MaViolet ate a little. She sipped at the water I brought. Her eyes lit up, and she surrounded me with questions: *You doing your best, Grandbaby,* she'd say. *You find something joyful yet this day?*

Knox and I claimed the glass-faced greenhouse room that jutted from Thomas Jefferson's cabinet and library. We dragged a bedroll from the floor above and made a padded place to lie beneath the windows. Those windows that opened tall as doors and looked onto the terrace and over Mulberry Row.

Five cloistered days, we explored Jefferson's

little mountain. Uprooted as we were, we filled those first days with discovery. We found a green old-timey carriage with giant black wheels, near the upper gift shop. We found the carcasses of a den of baby foxes in the pasture, their decaying bodies alive with flies. We found mice droppings along the low cellars and heard their plush and scurrying battalion advancing after dark. At dawn, a family of deer nosed up to our windows, necks elegant, ears low and fearless. We found a heap of downturned wheelbarrows entwined with vines. We untangled them and used them to cart things up the pale path past the welcome pavilion: bags of dried bean soups, lavender lotion, bottles of wine with a picture of the house on their labels. Soon we were making soups for supper, slugging saucers of wine while it lasted, with Ezra partaking zealously. On the second night, after dinner, I saw him stagger across the south lawn in the rain only to pee in the small muddy fishpond. We used boiling water, poured into basins, to wash our bodies and launder the clothing that we traded among us, so that I wore Knox's shirt for a day, and he wore Mr. Byrd's and so on. We opened up a locked storage shed and found old lawn equipment: chainsaws, mowers, a few precious canisters of gasoline.

On the third day, Georgie jogged up from the welcome pavilion to join us. He came on his own, wheelbarrowing a cache of snack bars he'd squirreled away. At the top of the hill, he relinquished his bounty to Ms. Edith's table, like an oath. I looked down the yard behind him, anxious or eager that Devin would be heading up too, along with Elijah. We had already sent down several shifts of guards to replace or buttress them, but Devin did not come up — not that day. I let myself feel relieved too, even if I missed seeing his face with its familiar contours.

Those first nights the sky would darken with rainfall so that the hazy light of the moon barely glimmered through. I'd lie beside Knox in our windowed room, feeling my stomach for some sign of change, one way or the other. I'd worry over MaViolet's breathing, listening for her sighing exhalations beneath the insistent thrum of rain. She only had that one half-used inhaler — but how easy it would've been for me to grab the others. My shame for failing to bring what she most needed smoldered in my chest. A gust of wind would rattle the windows, and I'd be up on my feet, mazing through furniture, to make sure she was not wheezing again. Whenever she asked, I'd shepherd her all the way through the house and down the narrow stairwell to the old privy bathroom, or — because she preferred them — to new toilets near the gift shop, which had so little natural light but were smooth and modern and familiar. I'd fumble with matches to light a candle, then afterward, I'd help her back to bed. Those nights, I hardly slept. But I know I slept some, because, more than once, I startled awake with some fresh and terrible vision flashing in my mind. One night, I heard men banging guns against the greenhouse window and when I looked out, I saw First Street again. A windowless van sat on the far side of the road and a group of grown men were dragging somebody toward it. They were dragging that teen, the one they'd bloodied when he ran out toward them. In sleep, all I could do was watch as they held him by his ankles, his armpits, as he bucked and called out, *Ma! Ma! Ma!* Whenever I woke, I knew those men *had* dragged that teen on First, for real, after striking him with their rifle. When I woke up, I remembered.

On our third morning in the house, Carol's hens offered up four perfect eggs. She brought them to morning rations in a basket she'd found, lined with cloth. *Are we waiting?* Carol asked again, looking back at Ira, who'd claimed a leather-backed chair. Ms. Edith surveyed the eggs, announcing we would crack them into our soup's salted boiling water that evening.

Waiting? Sure! Let's wait and wait, Ira said.

After breakfast, I found myself down below the long walkway of the southern terrace. Without thinking, I'd made my way to the windowless exhibit on the life of my namesake: Sally Hemings. Last summer, there'd been a video looping, projecting birds in flight onto a headless dress form and the wall behind. I stood for some time at the open-mouthed entrance, peering into darkness.

If we were waiting, I couldn't yet say what we were waiting for. Felt like Ms. Edith thought we were waiting for heaven. And LaToya, who'd spent a day sequestered in her room, appeared to be waiting for grace. When I brought a hot bowl of food to set by her door, she opened it abruptly, as if she'd been waiting silently on the other side to take it from my hands.

Ezra acted like we were waiting just to get it together so we could get back and make those men pay. He swore he'd gather all the boys and men near First Street, like the ones who lived in the yellow house next door to his daddy's house. *Somebody's got to pay,* Ezra said, upending our last bottle of wine, and looking down the dark path to the welcome pavilion. But for his brother's steadiness, Ezra probably would have gone back on his own.

Some wet and sweltering afternoons, when Ms. Edith came to sit with MaViolet, and if Knox was off addressing some issue with Mr. Byrd, I'd find myself on my own. I'd rove the house, its three floors and damp basement, its backroom docents' library full of books. I read because I've always read. I read to try to escape the tenuousness of our situation. I read to distract from the fact of my pregnancy, which was becoming more founded with each passing hour. How was it that I had ended up here, and knocked up, not knowing for sure who the father was? And what did it mean if Knox was the father, if Devin was? How had the world gotten so badly broken? I could feel my own jagged, rattling pieces reflecting light and dark, like a kaleidoscope.

To try to escape all that and more, I'd pull a book from the shelf and read by candle or window light. I read from Thomas Jefferson's *Notes on the State of Virginia,* running my fingers over his inventory of land mammals, his clever calculations of the heights

197

of the state's mountains, the depths of its rivers: a great and good man. I noted Jefferson's reflections on the mildness of Virginia's climate and thought of its ferocity now, the ways we'd desecrated our commonwealth. I read some of Jefferson's thoughts on human bondage. Slavery was "a moral depravity," he wrote, brutal to Black people and a means to make tyrants of white people. But then he also wrote that Blacks were inferior to whites, in body and mind, that we stank, that we were like children, unable to look after ourselves. And so, if slavery was to be ended, former slaves would have to be sent somewhere far away. Freed Blacks would *have* to leave, he concluded, because of the "deep rooted prejudices" of white people and the memory of Black people of the wounds they'd sustained at America's hand. These forces, Jefferson wrote, would "produce convulsions which will probably never end but in the extermination of the one or the other race."

I laid that book down and opened another, skimming the timeline of Jefferson's life — his inheritance from his father of the land I now stood on, his marriage to Martha and the births of his official children — those first, white children who would not be expected to prove and re-prove their lineage.

I imagined Momma's teacher looking down at eight-year-old Momma, not just disbelieving but repulsed. My own Momma had waited until late in life to have me, maybe because MaViolet had her too early, and with a man who did not love her after all. Momma was already in grade school by the time MaViolet married Papa Alred, who'd loved her like she was his own. Momma made no secret of my father's name, though I never knew him. He'd been, she assured me, good-natured and good-looking but only a friend to her, only a means to an end of having me, before it was too late.

I grew weary reading of Jefferson's life, so I searched out stories about Sally Hemings instead. Hemings, who was brought to Monticello as a child, along with her mother and siblings — a wedding gift of slaves from the father of the bride, like a set of silver platters. The accounts I found of Hemings were all secondhand, other people's words, so that it felt like the more I read, the more hidden she became. I discovered that Jefferson's father-in-law — the man who'd made a gift of her — was also Sally Hemings's father. This meant Sally Hemings was Thomas Jefferson's wife's half sister. How had it felt, I wondered, to be family and property all at once? And what did it mean to look on your owner and see sister? Or to look on sister and see slave? I read that most historians believe Jefferson first slept with Sally after Martha's death, while she accompanied the family to France to serve them. Jefferson was forty-one, Sally was fourteen. She came back from Paris pregnant at sixteen, with a promise from Jefferson that all of her children by him would one day be freed Black people. Jefferson and Hemings had six children together, four of whom survived into adulthood, living as slaves at Monticello until each one was eventually granted release.

In the end, none of Sally's released children felt safe enough to stay. Not Beverly, or Harriet, or Madison. Not Easton, who later published a memoir naming Thomas Jefferson as the patriarch of his family. Two Hemings children were allowed to walk off the mountain, slipping into obscurity and presumably living the rest of their lives divided from family and cloaked as white people. The other two eventually moved far out of state, in spite of Jefferson's written appeal to the general assembly that an exception be made for them. Years earlier there'd been an amendment borne of white people's fears about reprisal from freed slaves, after all the torment that had been heaped upon them. *And be it further enacted, that if any slave hereafter emancipated shall remain within this commonwealth more than twelve months . . . he or she shall forfeit all such right and be apprehended and sold.* Sally's children, once freed, remained dispossessed. Stay and we will find you and re-enslave you: Virginia is not your home.

VII.

It was the fifth morning when Devin finally came to the top of the hill, giving up his long stint at the welcome pavilion. When I saw him from the greenhouse window, I must've made some kind of sound. Knox looked up from whatever he was reading, the book I'd lent him or else his gridded notes. *You okay?* Knox said. In the yard, I could hear Mr. Byrd greeting Devin — *Young man!* — then the two of them speaking back and forth. I kept watching until I realized Knox was still waiting. *I am,* I answered.

As Devin followed Mr. Byrd along the path, I realized that his reluctance to come up to the house had not been entirely about me. There was a deep caution in the way he crested the terrace steps, his voice low as churchgoing. When he made his way inside to speak to MaViolet, he looked around as if in wary wonder at it all.

By contrast, Elijah bounded in a few minutes later, full tilt, bellowing out from the entrance hall. *Ezra! Where you at?* When Ezra galloped down, Elijah tackled his twin, a reunion of entwined limbs and bracing holds. A reunion of noogies like they were twelve or something. Someone whelped, someone pooted, and in the ensuing funk, the twins embraced in earnest, thumping backs, and then standing back to regard each other as if no legitimate tussle had happened. Like they'd been born to forgive each other. The twins settled in the third-floor room Ezra had chosen for them, with two beds against one wall. Devin chose an outcast space in the south pavilion, a brick room at the far bent end of the long plank-like terrace our greenroom opened up to. He would sleep as far away as possible from the main house and closer still to Mulberry Row.

It wasn't long before the first strangers showed up at the foot of our little mountain, but first, like a warning, the power fluttered on. It happened early, in the deep dark of our sixth morning, though each day here feels like a small, hidden lifetime. The power clicked and hummed, liberating whole sections of the house from darkness. We felt that seismic shift from thin pallets or lumpy beds, each of us listening for the thrum of things as they had once been. Knox bolted up beside me, his face half-lit by a lamp from the adjacent hall. His eyes looked naked without his glasses, and a dreamy smile unfurled across his face. Elsewhere I could hear murmuring, the kids stomping and cheering in the nursery above us, Georgie's satisfied curse from the front porch where he sometimes slept. As for me, I felt a knot in my stomach, as if to signal that something bad was coming for us along with that returning light.

It's coming back, Knox said, though the power lasted only a few ticking seconds. The brightness that flew into our room had flickered out by the time he spoke. I went to check on MaViolet — her room had held its darkness; I could hear her soft snores. Back in bed, Knox and I listened as the house settled to hushed whispers. I could feel him through the cocoon of darkness, his face intent, his body edging itself along mine. He pulled himself over me, holding his own weight on his elbows. I might've been breathing hard already. I know I tucked my body under his. Focused now, he dipped his face toward my face, like lowering himself down into water, something both desired and necessary. It's been like this between us since the first time we touched: I wanted something in him, or from him, or him from me — a surrender of distance, maybe. That night though, tears rolled sideways down my cheeks, collecting in my ears. Fear or something like it bleeding through my want.

We hadn't done it properly in weeks, not since right after spring break when those first heavy storms hit us. I'd stopped us because we'd run out of protection, and because I'd finally remembered myself after that brief, reckless time of forgetting. I'd stopped us because everything around us was crumbling, and because — ironically — I'd realized that I'd missed my period. I told Knox we had to be more careful, as if this responsible choice could unwind my earlier irresponsible ones; like I were begging some higher power, Pretty please let me not be pregnant after all. I'd kept up this prohibition even after it was clear it had not worked. That night when the lights pulsed back on, I knew I had to tell him. I should have told him right away.

Instead, Knox and I reached for each other, offering what pleasure we knew we could, with our mouths, our hands, our bodies rocking close. Knox brushed the tears from my cheeks. He must've imagined them as full of hope.

The first strangers showed their faces a few hours later, that same morning.

Per our rotation, Mr. Byrd, along with Ira and Carol, were taking their shift down at the welcome pavilion. They carried big walkies, a handgun, and both remaining shotguns. They carried a weird expectant feeling since the lights had flashed. It was daybreak when they saw a man with amber skin coming slowly up the road. He came with raised hands and wet leaves in his hair: a tree man, Carol later told me. He spoke with an accent, calling out across the distance even as Mr. Byrd and Ira fumbled to level their weapons. It felt impolite, Carol explained, to aim a weapon at a person trying to tell you who they are.

My name is Norberto Flores, the tree man said.

Arms still raised, he explained that his family had seen the smoke of our cooking fires. They'd seen our lights flash and watched what they could of us from a tree-lined path that cut through the forest below. The woods, the road — it was becoming more dangerous each day, the man said. *We watched and decided you all were not more dangerous.*

We soon learned that Mr. Flores, along with his grown sons and their families, had driven their camper from town after a disturbance near their home. Turned out they lived around the bend from Devin, on the other side of the trash-strewn gully behind the basketball courts. They were, essentially, our neighbors, and had seen smoke pouring up from First Street the night we fled. That same group of armed men had driven up and down their road, brandishing torches. One bearded man had shouted ugly things through a megaphone as Mr. Flores and his family huddled or fumed behind dark windows. The Flores family had left early the next morning, locking doors, securing all they could secure. They'd left in their Ford Sherrod, the old van full of tents and hunting gear. They'd driven toward the edge of town, taking the same route we'd taken, parking and hiking up to camp high above the Saunders-Monticello Trail, which runs alongside the road we'd turned onto the night we fled. But then, Mr. Flores explained, his family had begun to see armed groups of men below their encampment in the early evenings. *Los arsonistas,* Mr. Flores called them. Because of those men, his family no longer felt safe in the woods or driving along the road. The Floreses had gathered all they could carry, not knowing where to go, exactly. They'd hiked the path away from town and then they'd seen our lights.

When I heard all this, my fear ticked way back up, a frantic throbbing at my throat. Oh God, I thought, it's not safe in town, but it's not safe on the road either. Still, I pushed the fear deep down, until I could hardly feel it, at least not as something separate from me.

By the time Knox and I had jogged down to the welcome pavilion, Mr. Flores had retrieved his sons, Edward and Oscar, from the woods below, along with their wives, and his elfin teenaged granddaughter: all those generations descended from him, but born in Virginia — in the case of his sons, in the Valley near Harrisonburg. The family sat soberly along the benches near the ticket office where we'd once sat, their heads drooping, their expressions marked by a mix of bitterness and gratefulness I knew well. Large duffels, tents, sleeping bags, and hunting gear lay in a neat line near the ticket office. Beyond the pavilion, rain funneled from gutters, glazing the asphalt of the lot. As soon as I saw the Flores family, I knew we would not turn them away.

Not three days later, another group of strangers arrived, five young people in all. They showed up wearing cotton and spandex and denim beneath clear plastic rain ponchos. They showed up with red bandanas encircling their collars or else pulled up and halving their faces, as if they'd gotten lost on the way to a demonstration. Academic backpacks turtled their backs.

I was on duty with Elijah and LaToya — who'd begun to come out from her room more regularly, but who'd kept a listlessness about how she moved her body. When that second group reached us, it was the first and only time I'd ever leveled a gun at a person. To me guns meant indiscriminate power, the risk of fatally misjudging someone else's worth.

My hands shook. The rain blurred my vision.

The group revealed themselves as a single voice, amplified but trembling: *Do not be alarmed! We are SCFP — Students of Color for Peace! Are you friends or enemies of the people?* That deep voice cutting through rainfall belonged to a college sophomore named Lakshmi, a curvy copper-colored girl with a striking downward slant to her mouth. She'd tied her red bandana over her hair, half-shorn and glossy black. She drew the megaphone back to her lips. *You should know that some very bad things are happening down there! For fuck's sake, let us in.*

The students were part of a fledgling activist group from the same community college down the road that I'd attended for two years. They shared an apartment right behind campus, behind the man-made lake. Their school had shut down, chaotically, they told us — the cafeteria raided, the administrative offices strewn with papers. From their apartment, Lakshmi and the others had heard all kinds of rumors: that storefront windows had been smashed at Fifth Street Station, with people taking what they wanted or needed. That prisoners at the regional jail had died from hunger strikes or rioting in response to the 24/7 lockdown in unlit spaces. That there were plans for a large demonstration, demanding support from local and state government for those struggling to survive. But when the students had hiked downtown at the allotted time and peered from the bridge down to City Hall, no one was there.

Lakshmi and the others told us that they would walk some nights to the bottom of the driveway to their hillside campus. From a building near the road, they began to see small caravans of men, in SUVs and trucks, driving up and down the main road near the exits for the highway, laying on horns. They recognized the men — with their spectacle of flags and guns — as part of the same group they'd aimed to stand up to long before the grid crashed. They told us that the line of vehicles would roll by every night, right before dark. They'd loop around and either drive back toward town or else pull into a side street across the divided road. One time, Lakshmi and the others snuck closer, crouching near their side of the road. At sundown, when the caravan passed, Lakshmi said they'd seen what looked like bodies, beneath blankets, in one of the truck beds. They'd seen a foot flung out, but no, it had to have been an ax head or the barrel of a gun. The group had heard a rumor that there were local people up at Monticello, Black people. I wondered who had told them about us. Had Mr. Odem, the old white guard, told someone, who'd told someone else?

After the power flared in their apartment, the students told us that the road below campus had gone quiet again. A few days later, they set out to find us, in broad daylight, because the men always came at night. We were lucky, they told us, to be on this mountain, in this house. It was a refuge.

■ ■ ■ ■

It felt both comforting and trying, having all those new bodies up on the mountain: everything theirs too. More hands to chip in, but our rations spread thinner. We met all together that eighth night and the next, to recite our parchment rules, but also to pen in a few new ones. Anyone was free to leave with one day's rations. Anyone could be asked to leave if the group agreed. The Flores family had set up their tents in the parlor, sliding back red-cushioned chairs; they shuttled tent poles through nylon loops as the oily eyes of lurid portraits watched. Lakshmi and the other students went up to the house's third level, fashioning pallets on the dull green floor of the dome room.

The Flores family and the SCFP students brought new things onto the mountain:
a solar stove
low-light binoculars
a trio of hunting rifles
a massive crossbow with neon quivers
paper face masks and a dozen canisters of Mace
a set of hand-drawn zines touting tactical self-defense
Lakshmi and the other students taught us

hand signs they'd learned from fellow activist circles. Soon LaToya fell in with the students, gesturing agreement with snapping fingers, dry laughter rising in her throat. She swapped her gold-colored T-shirt with the only boy in their group, a rail-thin freshman named Gary Chen who had ivory skin and shaggy blue-streaked hair. I heard Gary lament to LaToya about his new boyfriend, found and lost in a matter of months. During a break in the storms, this boyfriend had driven home to Northern Virginia, "just for a few days," but had not returned. One morning, as we doled out rations — sweetened pecans, torn greens, and foiled squares of dark chocolate — Gary leaned in toward me. *Can you believe it,* he said, *I finally fall in love, I come out to my parents, and then the world explodes.*

In the evenings, after we sang, the Flores family and the new students shared their stories of town, and we recounted ours, mumbling or shouting or laughing to the point of tears. Afterward we'd collapse to sobs on the rough slate floors of the all-weather pass. Afterward KJ and the Yahya children would sprint off through the muddy yard toward the small exhibits below the south terrace. We'd find them clanking copper pots, conjuring a fake fire in the

deep hearth of the former slave kitchen.
We'd find them whimpering in the cave of
the Sally Hemings display. They'd be holding their knees, rocking, complaining that
their heads, their backs, their bellies hurt.

We were gathered one night on the sheltered northern porch when Devin spoke up.
He and I had kept our distance since he'd
come to the house, but whenever I saw him,
my eyes caught on his figure. Devin told the
story of the day he'd come home to find
that his uncle had passed. Devin said he'd
been in Prospect overnight, and I imagined
he'd gone to see some girl, though he
might've gone to trade for batteries, for
smokes. Whatever it was, when he got near
his house, he could tell something had happened, the way Ezra and Elijah were standing in the yard as he approached, leaning
over shovels. He saw what looked like a
body, on the side deck, beneath a white
sheet. I knew that deck, its wobbly wooden
banister, the urn-like planter by the door
that held plastic peonies so long ago sun-
bleached they looked nostalgic. By then,
there were no longer ambulances. There
were no longer funeral homes, not any that
Devin knew of. Devin said the only glim-
mer of hope had been the boys and men
who stayed in the yellow house next door,

who soon came over, mazing past spare tires and engine parts. The way Devin told it, I could see them too: brown-skinned boys in low jeans wearing colorful sneakers. White T-shirts hanging from their back pockets like lowered flags. After Devin shared this, he looked right at me for the first time after so much time of not looking. And I wanted to say something to comfort him. Because, after losing Momma, I knew that kind of hurt. Devin told us that the yellow-house men had relieved him and the twins of their shovels, taking turns, digging quickly, until they could lower his uncle's body into red Virginia clay.

As we tugged our chairs closer, out of the slanted reach of rain, Lakshmi spoke. She shared how she'd driven to her parents' place out in the county, in Albemarle. Her folks had retired a year earlier, relocating to a newly built three-story on a lone rural cul-de-sac — the sole brown family in a cluster of white ones. It was tranquil there, Lakshmi said, most of the neighbors had stayed put. And while she was there, she'd heard more than one neighbor knock at her parents' door to ask, Did they need anything? Lakshmi's parents had stockpiled wholesale-club supplies, vibrant spices, and enormous jars holding split lentils and dried beans.

One pantry shelf dedicated to bulk packs of peanut brittle clusters — her dad's weakness. Her mom still had hope for the wet-footed garden, and they'd all be fine there for the time being, her parents assured her. And it had been entirely peaceful on their street except for one dry evening, when a neighbor had come out shouting from his dark front porch — a retired widower, drunk maybe. By flashlight, he'd hung one of the old flags high from the post on his lawn, replacing the sodden American one. But this was the same neighbor who'd helped Lakshmi's parents when they first moved in, offering jumper cables when their battery failed, pulling his car up beside theirs even though the angle was awkward. Besides, her parents assured her, the lonesome man had taken that flag back down, somberly, the following night.

It was safe enough at her parents' place, Lakshmi conceded, but she had not stayed for long. On the way there, along one of those snaking rural routes, a pair of the men had blocked her passage. Not the same men who'd driven dark trucks past campus — but who could tell for sure anymore, Lakshmi said. The men who barred her did not show guns or flags or carry torches. One of them might not have been "white" — his

215

skin was an olive-tan. Either way, the men's car obstructed the road, and they'd propped their hood up, so that Lakshmi would have had to swerve into the ditch or plow into the car to get past. *I wish I'd run those fuckers over,* she said, adjusting her bandana, now knotted around her wrist. Instead, she'd stopped her Civic in the road, to ask them to move, or if they needed help. The men had made her get out of her car and sit in the back of theirs as they rifled through her things. Then one of the men had climbed into the back seat with her. *They took what they wanted,* she said, picking at the thick red knot.

Eventually they'd let her pass and she'd made it to her parents' house, but it had been too quiet there. After a couple nights, she'd used the last of her gasoline to drive back to town, returning to their dark apartment, to her roommates, despite her parents' protests. Coming back, she'd taken a different route, telling herself that if she saw men in the road again, this time she'd plow right through.

With each new story, my heart swelled in my chest until it felt colossal. It ached for Gary Chen, with his sapphire-streaked hair, because he seemed so clearly in love. And for Mr. Flores after he shared how he'd

216

emigrated from Honduras, many years ago. He'd survived a massive hurricane — the power had gone down there too, he told us; the winds had reduced his neighborhood to rubble. My heart surged for Lakshmi, for whatever had happened to make her leave the relative safety of her parents' place and move back into danger, as if danger had already staked its flag in her. Sometimes my heart felt so heavy and bruised, I could hardly move, or speak.

The next morning, at rations, Ms. Edith suggested that the ladies and girls meet all together. *An ounce of prevention,* she said as she dried her hands on a square of cloth on her lap. We met in the parlor, with its windows draped in faded crimson valances. We met while the Flores men collected wood, while Mr. Byrd and Knox worked to erect rabbit-proof barriers around key parts of the garden. We met while Ira and Georgie tended a fire with laundry boiling in a basin above it. While Elijah and Papa Yahya shuttled a ball made of plastic bags and rubber bands back and forth with Jobari and KJ along the all-weather pass. While Devin and Ezra and Gary kept guard down below. Edith came into the parlor from the western porch, shedding her borrowed boots, the treads clogged with chunks of dark, wet earth. She showed up holding Carol's cloth-lined basket, brimming with tiny strawberries and humble wilting flowers, leaves, roots, and all. *I aimed to bring something sweet,* she said.

We leaned in over the wooden floor, a tessellation of flat, smooth diamonds.

Ms. Edith made her way to each of us, pushing back a chair here, a small table there. We took a bit of fruit to our palms, a cluster of delicate flowers, balanced by tiny clinging roots. *Wild violets, go on.* She placed a pinch of leaves and flowers in her mouth, chewing.

We were Mama Yahya with the baby in her arms, and Imani, who wore fresh braids and a long gift-shop T-shirt, belted like a dress. We were Lakshmi and her cohort: Mahreen, Kayla, and Jia. We were the Flores women, Sam and Marta, along with Marta's elfin thirteen-year-old daughter, Yamileth.

We were silver Carol and rose-gold La-Toya.

We were me.

I held tart sweetness on my tongue, saving the rest in my palm for MaViolet, who still lay in that bed a room away from us.

Ms. Edith stood near the window, narrowing her eyes on the sodden oval beds in the yard. *Larkspur, calendula, lenten rose.* She looked us up and down. *You ladies know we've got to be careful,* she said. And Imani — who stood beside her mother — clutched her stuffed woolly mammoth. The six-year-old was confused, we hoped, though the rest of us knew just what Ms. Edith meant. *Real careful,* Ms. Edith went on, *even now, especially now. Matter-fact, we ought to be careful any time, all the time.*

I rocked deeper into my velvet seat, as if that owl-eyed woman were channeling Momma's old admonitions. *It's been like this for women and girls, on and on, all the way back to creation,* Ms. Edith said.

The rest of us uh-huhed or nodded, even me — a general cry of assent. We looked at each other, then out the windows where rain cast dripping shadows. The Yahya baby stretched along his mother's lap, extending tiny grasping hands.

When he began to fuss, Mama Yahya rocked her legs to soothe him, a movement that generally escalated to her standing and jiggling and singing, except this time Imani, whose face suddenly beamed with sisterly pride, abandoned her soft beast on a table and reached for her baby brother instead. Once she held him in her arms, cradling his head, he hiccupped. His cries subsided for a while.

We've got to look out for one another, Ms. Edith said in her throaty voice.

LaToya changed the cross of her ankles. *Wouldn't that be something.*

Ms. Edith went on to petition us to use good sense, to protect ourselves and each other from the men we'd surely see whenever we went back, or from men who might end up at this house. She said we had to be careful even of the boys and men already on the mountain, our fathers and brothers. Our friends and lovers. If we stayed here long enough, Ms. Edith warned, there could be, and probably *would* be, moments of coercion, force even. This wasn't a time to get hurt or pregnant, if we could help it. She said this like she knew we might not be *able* to help it, and I wondered, had some trusted person hurt Ms. Edith along the way. At the word "pregnant," I bit the inside of my lip; a bubble rose in my throat.

Across the room, LaToya called out, *Amen!* like a brazen convert. And Lakshmi, who was already standing, rubbed her clump of flowers so brusquely the petals came apart.

The baby began to cry again, and Imani rocked urgently, humming a made-up song to a familiar tune. In patchwork English, Mama Yahya shared tips on how to handle our periods, a thing that I, unfortunately, no longer had to worry about. *Look out for yourselves and each other,* Ms. Edith concluded, and everyone drew in. Like we could. Like we would, even me. I pulled my knees up, rocking, swallowing my confession whole.

We'd been two weeks in the house when I woke to the sound of wheezing. It was nighttime, still deep dark, and Knox was dead asleep. I bolted upright, having heard or sensed that labored sound. Before I woke fully, I'd stumbled through the cabinet room — chair backs and the multiplying feet of furniture — to make it to MaViolet's boxed-in bed. My hands found her hands and I braced against the reedy whistle of her trying to capture air. I reached through the darkness for her inhaler — not sure how much, if any, medication remained. I'd kept it on her nightstand in a futile attempt to ward off its necessity. Now I shook it and brought it to MaViolet's mouth.

She worked at it for a moment then swatted it away.

When I was a kid, MaViolet had suffered an attack once when we could not find her inhaler. I'd run next door to our neighbor's for help, and soon enough red and white lights pulsed on our front windows. Other neighbors wandered into our front linked yards to try to see. The EMTs rolled Ma-Violet into the back of the ambulance and told Momma to follow. We scrambled for keys and jumped into Momma's beat-up Corolla, but I was gripped by dread. All I could think was, What if we break down? What if the ambulance loses us on the drive to the hospital? What if we never see Ma-Violet alive again? I worried if we weren't right there to beg the doctors to try, they might be careless with MaViolet's precious body. They might misjudge her endless worth.

In bed, MaViolet wrestled with her sheets, her mouth gulping at nothing. This is when I lose her, I thought.

I called out for help.

I shoved a pillow under her, rolling her onto one side.

Before I realized what I was doing, I'd crawled up into that high bed too. It felt hard beneath me, unforgiving as freshly packed dirt. I curled myself around my grandma's body, to try to comfort her, as if I could crawl into her skin. I sometimes used to sleep in her bed when I was little.

She'd seemed so big back then, vast spirit and broad chest, always emitting warmth. That night, breathless, in my arms, she felt too narrow, as if her bones had been whittled. A scattershot burst of rain hit the roof, followed by a strong wind — the house seeming to sway with it.

Wheeze, whine, wheeze, whine —

In this way, seconds or hours passed.

Then Knox was there and standing over the cabinet-room side of the bed, his hand hot on my back. He made me sit up, helped me to pull MaViolet to sitting so that her feet dangled. He prompted me to try once more with the inhaler. He made MaViolet sip at whatever was in the saucer on the bedside table — water or tea. Between rasping breaths, she choked a bit down, straining still. Straining less.

Much later, when the sky was alive with birdsong despite the rain, Ms. Edith came back, as always, to sit by MaViolet's bed. I was exhausted, grateful for a reprieve, though I knew I would not be able to sleep. I found Knox on the terrace outside our room's open window, his lanky body pitched against the brick exterior arch. His shirt, washed and worn again, looked thinner, the stripes across his chest faint. His hair, usually so neat, had grown out shaggily since the storms. He turned at the sound of my approach and I dredged up a smile for him, because MaViolet had survived the night, and because he'd smiled when he saw me, that old dreamy smile, if fleeting. In his haste to help, he must've dropped his glasses the night before. They looked like they'd gotten bent and reshaped; they made a new geometry of his cheeks.

Your name, I said, an imitation of the first night we met, across a table, with me marking his name on a tag. But my voice came out flat, even though I'd tried to infuse it with air.

Knox, he answered, sitting up straighter. *What's yours?*

Da'Naisha, I said.

When I got close enough, he reached out to loop me into his arms, and pulled me toward him as if in slow motion, his chest sticky with heat. When I looked up, he was gazing far off at the ridge of low blue mountains. Just as slowly, with intention, he untangled himself, moving back to look at me.

I guess I don't understand, he said.

I thought at last Knox would say something murky and true about me — about how I'd neglected to bring what MaViolet most needed, or how he sensed my unfaithfulness in the way Devin and I avoided one another. I nearly hoped he'd finally say he'd noticed my body's soft revolution: the pregnancy I'd worked to keep hidden but that must've been showing itself in small ways. At that moment, I wanted him to say something shameful about me. But Knox only spoke of the world and its failings. The problems that desperately needed solving, and how they might be solved. *There are people who can fix this, Da'Naisha,* he said.

Why didn't I just grab her medication, I remember saying.

Smart people, Knox persisted. *People more than capable of restoring the lights, getting the planes back in the air. My father even — he's brilliant. But there are other people, better people, groups who could come up with a plan to temper the worst of this weather we've made.*

It had to have been in the kitchen, I said. *Or else on her bedroom dresser.*

We're probably just in some terrible bubble, Knox said. *I bet there are people working to get here, to town, I mean. It's awful, this moment, but it's probably fine elsewhere, in Maryland or in West Virginia. Hell, maybe it's fine in Richmond. We can't see it now, because we're inside it. But this has got to be an aberration. It will be fixed. Then we can go back.*

You could go back to town, I said. *You should go.*

Are you listening to me? Knox said. *If things don't get fixed, your grandmother is going to die here!*

My body went flighty again, as if it was not nearly heavy enough to hold me, even if my bare feet remained squarely on the planked terrace. Behind me, in the house, I could almost feel MaViolet turning in her bed. I held my own arms, rubbing them, trying to wake my body up.

Da'Naisha — wait, Knox said, his Adam's apple rising and falling at his throat. *I'm sorry, honey,* he said.

You should go back, I repeated.

It's going to be okay, Knox said, as if he hadn't even heard me. Maybe my words were garbled. Maybe I was already speaking into the dirt. *I just mean it shouldn't all fall on you,* he said.

Knox kept saying sorry, his hands on my shoulders, my neck, pulling me to him. I could feel him kiss my earlobe, my jagged part, as he spoke: *You're going to become this incredible teacher. I'll get hired somewhere in town, nothing fancy at first, but*

226

something in energy — geothermal, wind. Knox had pulled my head to his chest and I could hear his heart thumping. *I'm just worried is all. What if nobody comes,* he said.

I looked out over at the sky, thick with fog, and the Afro-ed heads of trees nodding, and the dark depressions of roads. *More dangerous every day,* Mr. Flores had said, and the students had seen the men driving at night, near the highway, until they had stopped seeing them. I was so tired I could've collapsed onto the beaded wetness.

I pressed my mouth into Knox's chest. *What if somebody comes,* I said.

VIII.

When I opened my eyes, the light on the walls had shifted. I must've fallen back to sleep on my pallet because now it was fully day. I could hear muted footfalls around the house, the gentle creak of a door swinging. Someone called across the yard outside an open window. I lifted myself, made my way back to MaViolet's bed.

I could hear her steady breathing, and there was a smear of color on her cheeks. Maybe she'd been listening for me. As soon as I walked in, she opened her eyes and spoke.

Grandbaby, she said.

She looked fine. Better than fine, but for how long?

Nay-Nay, she said, brow furrowed like she was worried about *me.* I hugged her so hard, then opened all the windows. When I sat back on the edge of her bed, I wrapped my hands around her once more.

MaVi, I said, smiling like crazy just to see her alive, to hear her voice.

Sun's up, she said, and it was. The rain had stopped entirely. Outside the window I could see steam rising from the grass.

I asked if she'd been by herself for long, and she gestured toward Ms. Edith's chair. *Y'all keeping me in good company,* she said. The bed felt easier beneath me; still, I could feel grit in the sheets. MaViolet curled her arm around my waist, her cool palm slaking my skin.

You need anything? I ventured. *What can I get for you?*

That clock, she said, looking at Jefferson's timepiece mounted at the foot of her bed. It had a white face, golden gears, and swirly hands like cursive writing — its head suspended between two black obelisks. *My daddy carried a pocket watch,* she said. *Nothing fancy, mind you, but gold edged too.*

MaViolet had grown up in Vinegar Hill, in a two-story clapboard house with yellow

228

curtains in the windows. She used to talk about her old house sometimes, how it, along with her whole neighborhood, had been bulldozed to the ground about the same time she'd finished grade school, and all the Black families who lived there had been forced to move on. *My daddy was a prideful man,* she told me that morning. *Used to let me hold his golden watch, and my mother bought me patent leather shoes, with ribbons. It was a man's watch — heavy but pretty. I used to pretend it was mine.*

MaViolet wrenched her body up to try to get a better view out of the window. The day looked pale with sun.

How come you never talk much about your parents? I said.

I got pregnant, she said. *The summer I graduated. But you know that.*

I nodded, hoping she would keep talking.

Daddy actually wanted to see me go to college since he didn't have a son, she said. *He was right about one thing: your mother's father turned out to be no account. It was a while before I met Papa Alred — such a funny man — but I outlasted him too.*

You'll outlast us all, Grandma, I said. *We'll go home soon.*

You look so much like both of them, she

said. *Specially around the eyes: like your Momma, and like mine.*

It hurts, I said, struggling to swallow. *Sometimes I try not to think of Momma because of how bad it hurts.*

MaViolet's eyes were trained on the window. *When they brought us here last time,* she said, *it was spring.*

When Ms. Edith came — bringing food for MaViolet and standing at the window, the furrows of her face cracking open as she looked out at the kids running wild, the way the sun marked their bodies — I told her briefly what had happened with MaViolet the night before. Then I ducked down through the all-weather pass to the old privy, closing myself off in that dim space. I'd put on the plainest gift-shop T-shirt I could find and it hung loose over my body. But my cutoffs, which rode high on my stomach, had tightened around me in the intervening days, pressing a thin welt across my belly. I peered into the small hand mirror and admonished myself, slapping my cheeks, trying to wake myself. I should've told MaViolet then that I was pregnant. But how could I heap more worry on top of her worry? I knew her asthma could come back at any moment. And of course, Knox was

230

right: If nothing changed, the next time she might die.

In the yard, near the west porch, Carol was cleaning up from the morning meal. Devin stood beside her, washing dishes in a basin. *There you are,* Carol called out when she saw me. *You were supposed to do this.* She pushed a stack of dirty bowls across their table, toward me, but Devin glanced up, our eyes met for a moment. He pulled the dishes back. *I got this,* he said.

Everybody on the mountain worked harder than ever that fourteenth day, buoyed by the break in rain, I figured, fueled by the feel of sun on skin. They worked in small groups, in the yard or the house, straightening shared spaces. They dug with trowels for hidden root vegetables in the garden, and reached high into crooked branches for ripening fruit in the orchard below. Folks churned wash in basins, strained taut lines with wrung but dripping laundry, their backs bowed, their hands chapping. Afterward, they rubbed in the thick lotion Ms. Edith had found in the gift shop, that smelled of lavender. Folks kept watch too, a steady shift of two or three in a rotation at the welcome pavilion, holding weapons, and walkies, and borrowed grace. I was moved by all that effort, though in truth it felt misguided to me that day. Even so, I did my best to mimic the swing of their arms, the rhythm of their legs moving forward: their hope. I moved my mouth soundlessly when Mr. Byrd opened his to call out to Georgie, asking the younger man to bring the first aid kit down. I shuttled my arms along with Mr. Flores's movements, as he cleaned and oiled a line of guns in the grass, his expression reluctant, as if he'd been a pacifist in another life. I widened my eyes along with KJ, who sat on a step in the yard, his eyebrows and scar raising in tandem, in anticipation of pain before its arrival. Moments later, Mr. Byrd bent down to remove a splinter from the bottom of KJ's bare foot with a sewing needle. As I passed them, I caught a whiff of sulfur. *It's done — you can go on and play now, son,* Mr. Byrd said.

That evening, Lakshmi ladled out our bean soup supper on the covered west porch. Beside her LaToya and Gary portioned out salted nuts, raw carrots, colorful stalks of chard. Imani and Jobari had set up a small station with a basin of warm water and soap so that people could wash their hands before and soak their bowls after. By the time I got there, my hands were marked by fresh blisters, though I could not recall which action had raised them. Most folks were already settled, with bowls on their laps. Now that the rain had stopped, a few people had pulled chairs outside, borrowed from the parlor or entrance hall. Others sat along the porch steps. The Yahyas, along with Yamileth, sat on blankets in the grass. A couple of the students were guarding down below.

I'm going back to get my grandma's medication, I intended to say.

I could see Georgie coming over, scrambling around the fishpond and the giant willow oaks. Even before he got his bowl, he jumped headlong into a story, his chin tipping up, his voice vibrating with excitement. He'd just seen a group of brown bears — cubs, actually. Could we believe it? *A sloth of bears,* he said.

Ezra stood near a table, brought out to the lawn, gnawing at a bitter stalk. He announced he'd heard a baby crying. For real, down in the fields, the night before. And he'd heard it *after* the Yahya family had headed up to the nursery to bed.

Ms. Edith's teeth, the color of aged ivory, flashed briefly. *Haunts,* she said.

Nothing but a baby fox, Mr. Byrd said, taking a sip from his mug.

I was sitting beside Knox on those porch steps, brick edged and topped in slate. My legs so much darker than his, my feet bare and stretching toward the sprawling west lawn, my socks and sneakers flung out onto the grass. The Flores family had re-pitched their tents at the farthest end of that lawn, near the tree line. Inside, MaViolet was resting in the bedchamber; by all accounts, she'd gone quiet since that morning when she'd spoken so freely with me. Ms. Edith had told me that when she offered food, MaViolet had not taken even a bite.

Devin was eating too far across our loose circle, seated between the twins. He tipped back in the chair that held his body, his boots wedged against the overgrown grass. I noticed that Devin was looking around at everybody. He looked at Papa Yahya, who was hastening the children to stop playing around, to sit still on their blankets while they ate. He looked at Ms. Edith, who was cackling at something Mr. Byrd had just said. He scanned out past the edge of the lawn, as if to check for danger even though he was not on duty. The far tree line shone with the falling light, a million shades of greens.

It came out then, those words that had been forming all day and since the night before — maybe since the moment I stumbled up the steps of the east porch and heard MaViolet rasping: *I'm going back,* I said, rising to my feet.

I mean to get MaViolet's inhalers, I said. *She could hardly breathe last night —*

I could tell by their expressions they knew already what had happened with MaViolet. Maybe Knox had told them, or Ms. Edith. Maybe that's why, all day, it had felt like they were eyeing me with some mixture of pity and tenderness. As they worked at their suppers, folks began to talk about town, about what they wanted and what was safe, one voice weaving into the next.

Papa Yahya said, *We need more meat for the men!*

Lakshmi said, *Those men were up and down that road every night, but then, suddenly, they weren't.*

Elijah said, *We can't let Naisha's grandma die in the heat like a dog.*

Ira said, *They were right there, outside my own goddamn window — I kept looking, they kept coming.*

Ezra said, *I'm ready to go back and make somebody sorry.*

Ms. Edith rinsed her bowl and waved to the children to bring their dishes over too. Around us the sky had turned deep orange with purple at its edges.

Knox stood up then, on the step just above mine. He took off his glasses, worked to clean them with the edge of his shirt, then put them back on.

I could go, he said. *I could go and try to get her medication and see if town is safer. I can go tomorrow.*

There was more talk about the roving men below the Floreses' camp, and near the highway, but Knox persisted. Things were settling down, he said, or would be soon. In the meantime, he could go.

It's a risk, both ways, Mr. Byrd said. *Going and not going.*

Ira worked to pick something from his teeth with his thumbnail. *He wants to go — let him go!*

There was water running across the road, Georgie said. *Down near the cubs. Could be worse lower down —*

I'll go the day after tomorrow, then, Knox said.

I sat back down and Knox turned to touch my knee, promising, in a low voice, he could do this thing for me. Felt like he was mistaking my sullenness for worry, my small hot fury for gratitude. Or maybe it was my fault, the way I offered one wall after another, my face a stone slate. Whatever he saw in me, he addressed the group again.

I'm going, he said.

He could go, he would go. That contained livid thing flared at my center.

Carol stood abruptly from her chair beside Ira, her sterling spoon clanking against the ceramic mug that held the dregs of her soup. Silvery bangs fringed her eyes.

I could go too, Carol said.

Ira tugged on her sleeve. *Don't be ridiculous.*

No, Carol said, shaking him off. *You oughta listen to me.*

Carol made her case, her voice skittering at first. If she and Knox were stopped, they could pretend to be mother and son, she suggested. *Just look at us — anyone would want to help us.* She went and stood on the other side of Knox, leaving Ira to pooh-pooh her plans from a distance. Side by side, they did look sympathetic: Carol with her sloping shoulders, and Knox, tall and bookish.

I want to do something good, Carol said.

Ira sat his empty mug on the grass next to hers.

Over rinsed dishes, and melty savored squares of chocolate, it was decided: Knox and Carol would go — both of them — because their skin would likely keep them safe. They'd leave the morning after next, at first light, since the armed men seemed to always come as the day was ending. They would go so long as the roads looked clear and the storms held off. They would take Mr. Byrd's Lincoln Town Car, the tank topped off with some of the gas we'd discovered in the shed of lawn equipment. Knox would drive and Carol would take note of everything she could about the old neighborhood. Even Devin said it made some kind of sense. Even Ira gave in, his hands trembling around the cup of tea Ms. Edith had extended to him. He promised to take care of Carol's precious hens until she returned. Carol was worried about predators, hawks in particular. *I'll mind those goddamn birds,* Ira said, gruff voice breaking to expose a kernel of doting pride.

After supper, I was scheduled for duty down at the welcome pavilion. That was the night I came across yet another stranger, at the edge of our woods. I was on guard with Knox and Edward Flores, who had the same firm but gentle demeanor as his father. As always, we took shifts, with one of us waiting near the ticket office with a walkie while the others patrolled the perimeter of the parking lot and the woods down to the entrance at the road. On duty, we'd round that humble slave burial ground, the one Mama Yahya had unwittingly led me to. We'd meet back at the ticket office to confirm everything was secure.

While Knox and Edward took their separate rounds, I leaned against a wooden column, my eyes burning. I was so exhausted that my mind kept taking off from one place to another. It flew to MaViolet, who'd gone quiet again, though before my shift, she'd taken a few sips of water. I knew I should be up by her bedside, but I was terrified to hear that long rasp again, and what would I do if I heard it? I'd asked Ms. Edith to sleep there while I was on duty. She'd pursed her lips but said okay.

I had one of Mr. Flores's shotguns slung across my back, the strap at a slant, cutting my chest in two. Earlier that day, I'd asked the older man to show me how to hold and aim and shoot. The secret, Mr. Flores had said, was in your head and your heart, not in your hands. I'd squinted at a target balanced out past the red-roofed stable, and when I felt a painful kick, my stupor lifted: For a moment, I'd remembered the weight of my body.

My mind flew to Knox, who was patrolling the lot. When he'd volunteered at dinner to go to town, I knew he wanted to protect me, to help me, yet he seemed unable to see me. Or maybe I didn't want him to. Maybe I was scared to let him see the broken bits, the sharp and jagged pieces. Could he accept those parts too, love them even, given the past we'd inherited, which now felt like future? Could I?

My mind hovered above Devin, looking down on him from a safe distance, his figure walking Mulberry Row, his tawny boots crushing pebbles. Had I imagined him looking at me earlier that day — his small act of kindness? Why did I care so much either way? I pushed Devin out of my head, and there, in his wake, Momma appeared, laid out in a dress the color of lemons, gray-faced and too young for that coffin. *Momma,* I tried, but my voice broke. I pinched the inside of my arm. It was better this way, I told myself, that she'd been spared this fearful, exiled waiting.

Finally, my thoughts settled on the being inside me, trying to stitch itself into a person — *a girl!* And was I even eating enough for her? What kind of world would she be born into — a sick, sick world. What kind of mother could I hope to be in a world as broken as this?

Knox came back from his patrol, unwind-

240

ing from his gun strap and hugging me easily. *All's quiet,* he said. Then it was my turn to walk and his to wait.

It was so hot that night, even the chatter of insects felt suppressed. When we'd first arrived, the moon had been full, if hazy, but that night it shone slimly, a sliver glowing white above me. I walked down into the woods and was more than halfway to the road when I saw the stranger, a shadow between the line of trees. He was on our side of the road, facing town; his presentation felt so different than the others who'd come before him, with raised arms and raised voices — those others who were part of us now.

I blinked and saw that he was just a boy, ten or eleven. His flashlight, dim to begin with, flickered and bobbed in his hand. As I watched, he stopped to peer into the rising woods as if he were looking right through me. Our Monticello, I remember thinking. I sank to one knee, my body braced like a buttress, my heart leaping and rearing back. He began to mount the slope between us, coming closer, then halting again. He crouched and that was when I saw something known in his profile. He was using his flashlight, fussing with a knapsack he carried, and the path of his eyes rose up toward the house, and all it held that was precious to me. His gaze slipped back, and that was when he saw me, kneeling in the woods and looking down at him. He was close enough that the light of his flashlight stung my eyes.

The thing was, I *knew* that boy, I thought I knew him. It was that same boy I'd seen jeering from the pickup window, the one who'd haunted my dreams. I don't know what my face did when I saw him. I only know what his face did in reaction to mine. His eyes went wide and his mouth fell open. There was a fearful lurching backward and down the slope he'd only just begun to climb. I felt my body in motion too.

I thought I would fly out toward him and shout, Keep going! Instead, my mouth seized, I lost purchase, and sliding, something sharp bit my ankle. A line of fire ran along my hip. The boy seemed desperate in his retreat, but I kept after him, half stumbling until my feet found the reliable flatness of road. After that, I ran in earnest, my sneakers slapping the glittery asphalt, the borrowed rifle knocking at my spine. The boy was fast, but I was faster. I didn't realize I could be *that* fast. The distance between us collapsed to nothing. I lunged and caught the flap of his knapsack. He went down hard and howling.

I only meant to hold and shake him. But then his weight was pinned beneath mine, my knees sinking into his narrow chest. My arms raised themselves and I could feel every ounce of my body, as my fists gaveled down on the boy on the road. *Who are you! I shouted. Who the fuck do you think you are?*

I kept on shouting — it's a wonder no one heard me — my words a series of frantic notes, almost like a refrain.

The boy's cries dissolved into a kind of helpless grunting, a sound like recognition, acceptance even. Those lower animal sounds finally brought me back to myself. My hands fell heavily to my sides. I moved off his body, my breath heaving, my whole body alive with tremors. He lay in the road like he might never get up. He looked smaller from that intimate distance, younger, his face dark with blood. But it was that same boy; it had to be.

Finally, this child fumbled for his bag. He got up, stumbling back and away from me, slowly at first, before turning to run down the road toward town. I watched him get away, standing out past our stretch of woods, farther out than I'd been in many days.

By the time I made it back to the welcome pavilion, I could hardly speak. I must've still been shaking, my clothes crooked on me, my hair wild in places, but there was hardly any moon left. Edward was waiting, his eyes dipping closed. *All's quiet,* I said.

IX.

I woke alone feeling nauseated. The sun sat fat and high in the sky outside of our greenhouse windows. I moved quietly through the house, passing the cabinet room, through which I could see MaViolet's back rise and fall. I moved through a narrow hallway and down the airless stairwell. At the open door near the cutouts of house slaves, I glimpsed a group of SCFP students in the stuffy dimness of the docents' library. Gary holding court, a hardback splayed in his hands. LaToya beside him, gesturing like a game show hostess. He recited something in a staid professor voice, and the others laughed desperately. I slinked past their view, moving through the rough walls of the all-weather pass, toward the covered place where we took turns boiling water. The fire was out, but the water still felt warm. I filled a bucket and brought it with me into the old privy.

That bathroom stank of urine, of shit, even though we doused it in boiled water and tried to keep it clean. I bent to peer into the old handheld mirror, feeling like I might see a different person looking back at me. My face looked just the same — I had to pull back clothing and angle the mirror to locate the evidence. A thin scratch along my collar, a graying bruise on my arm. I shed my T-shirt entirely and stepped out of my filthy shorts. Faint steam rose from my bucket. I stood naked and shivering in the heat.

I ran my hand over the deep scrape along my hip and recalled the sensation of sliding. The muscles of my arms ached, but my belly remained a narrow lie. Who was the boy — who did he think he was? I shook the tight squeeze from my hands and unfolded one of the squares of fabric we kept there to wash up.

I dunked the rag into my bucket of tepid water, used it to wipe my face, my neck, my chest, my armpits. I wiped the broken skin on my hip and ankle. I wiped between my legs, between my toes. I stepped back into my rank clothing and walked out into the sun.

Out in the yard, the full heat of the day hit me, as if the air itself was a massive object to navigate. Hottest springtime on record, they'd said on the news, back when there'd been news. I wondered, was it summer yet, officially? And what would that season bring for us if we made it to summer? Summer in Virginia without AC, or antiperspirant. Without the water park on Cherry, or melty pops in their thin plastic sleeves. Summer without a breeze through a moving car's window, or the hypnotic tick of the fan in Knox's dorm room. Already I could feel sweat swamping my armpits, my chest. Back upstairs, I checked in on MaViolet: Her eyes were squeezed closed, her breath heavy but steady-sounding. I made myself sit near her bed a while, though I couldn't bear to sit there long. And what was I doing to help her? I looked up at the oddly placed window above me, casting light and shadow on the ceiling. Not once as I sat there did MaViolet open her eyes.

As I moved through the rest of that sweltering afternoon, I saw the twins, down at the tree line, lugging a large fallen branch. I saw KJ and Jobari on their knees, in the dirt, and Imani a few rows over, twirling. I saw Ms. Edith in a chair in the shade, showing Yamileth how to set a straight stitch. In their small, exhausted motions, I could feel my own wrath burning off. Oh God, I thought. He was just a kid. What am I doing? What have I done?

Da'Naisha, someone said.

It was Carol, up on the west porch. My name always felt forced, the way she said it. *Would it be too much trouble?*

She was carrying a tall set of bowls, and at the same time, a bucket of utensils. The day had flown by me. The sun was beginning to sink, blazing treetops. It was almost suppertime again.

Let me get that, Knox said, coming up from behind me. I'd kept my eyes down, avoiding him that day as much as I could. He squeezed my shoulder before freeing the bucket from Carol's grasp.

After we ate that evening, folks began to recount preparations for the coming day. Mr. Byrd and Devin had gotten the Town Car ready, checking the tires and making sure it started easily. Georgie had surveyed the roads below to see if they looked clear of brush and water. Ms. Edith had collected a list of house numbers, drawing and labeling a map of that loop from First Street to the twins' house, and around to where the Floreses lived. Knox held the map out so that Carol could study it with him, trailing the route to town and back. I nodded, though I knew it wasn't entirely safe: Part of me knew.

I know y'all are going, I heard myself announce to the group. *I guess that makes sense. But I'm going too.* When I said this aloud, I felt relief.

I felt like I had to go because I alone was sure to get my hands on MaViolet's medication. But also, I needed to lay eyes on our duplex, if it still stood. I needed to see MaViolet's shelving unit, her lifetime of collections. Somewhere toward the middle shelf was a photograph of all of us: MaViolet and Momma and me. Some Easter morning long before I knew Momma was sick, before I knew mommas could even get sick enough to leave you by dying. In the picture, we are a trinity of pastels with Momma in the middle, her white leatherette pocketbook swinging on a golden chain. Felt like MaViolet's place was *our* dwindling family's museum, and I *needed* to see it, as walls or ashes, one more time.

Ezra said if *I* was going, *he* should go. He dreamed about finding those men every single night.

You too hot-headed, Elijah said. *Hell, if you go, I go.*

Why y'all always talking about going back there? KJ said.

Devin stood up and spoke and all our eyes went to him. I saw his mouth flare open, that golden glint if you knew where to look. *We've got to talk and listen,* he said. *We've*

248

got to work together.

Even after he'd sat back down, he kept our attention.

And Naisha prob'ly should go, Devin added.

I was smart, he said, and stubborn, and would make certain I got the meds if they could be gotten. And I'd had the sense to bring us here, he said. Apparently Ezra told him that MaViolet and I were descendants of Monticello. *We've been living up and around town and in these counties, like we've got no stake in it at all. Like we're vagrants or something,* he said. *Hell, who knows who my momma's people were, who my daddy's people were, way back. Chances are, they gave this land their blood, sweat, and tears, and those who owned them profited.*

Before he'd been sent to live with his uncle, Devin had started with a solid tripod of a family: a momma *and* a daddy *and* a pretty brick split-level, not far from the high school. It had been the most ordinary stresses that toppled them, just as he entered teen-hood: a job loss, untended depression, a violent event. The solution of sadness and anger must have seeped into Devin's ten- and eleven- and twelve-year-old body. By the time I started to see him around First Street again, his mouth held a different kind of quiet, though a bit of his old gentleness always shone through when we were alone together.

It's a risk, Devin concluded, *but if Naisha feels like it's got to be her, if she only trusts herself to do it, then she should go.*

The map rustled in Knox's grasp, and I could the see the calculations tensing his cheeks.

I don't know, Knox said.

She should go, Devin persisted.

I'm going, I said.

The light kept shifting. Blinking, we let our eyes adjust.

Then Devin said that *he* was going too. The twins would protect everybody, he said; they were tough, big-hearted, and should stay at the house, together. But he and I would go with Carol and Knox to get the meds and see about town.

We'll go and be back in a heartbeat, Devin said.

All those days on the mountain, and Devin and I had done our best to avoid each other. But that night, it was decided: Devin and I would both go, early the next morning, along with Knox and Carol. But Devin and I would be hidden in the trunk, because our skin made us dangerous. That night I lay awake, listening to the trill of insects, wondering if I should call it off. If I backed out, would they all still go without me? What if something happened to Knox, or Carol, or Devin, while I'd stayed safely behind? And what if they went, got all the way to First Street, but failed to bring back Ma-Violet's medication? I went and sat next to MaViolet's bed, speaking softly into the dark. *I miss home, I miss home, I miss home, I miss home, I miss home.* MaViolet did not answer. Her face looked newly twisted in sleep.

We set out early the next morning, before the break of day.

Legs shaky beneath me, I followed Knox out of our boardwalk terrace, then down the stairs toward Mulberry Row where we fell in with everybody: Mr. Byrd and the twins. Ira and Carol. Devin came last, jogging toward us from somewhere near the fish pond. He was wearing a plain T-shirt he'd likely swapped with Ezra, the bright white glowing against his skin. The straight brick path ahead unspooled before us, seeming to disappear between the black bodies of the trees.

Looking back over my shoulder, I could see Monticello's dome, shadowy against the dawning morning. Beneath it, on the west lawn, the bubbles of the Flores family's tents shone softly, along with the flare of laundry strung between trees. Down the slope to the garden, limbs trembled beneath the skittish orchestration of finch feet. Our tools edged the red-brown pathways, everything lauded by the chirrup of birdsong. Such a short time here and look how industrious we'd been — our threadbare striving! We'd go to town, I told myself, we'd get MaViolet's medication and we would all come safely back. When we got back, I would work harder for *all* of it: food, shelter, safety. Life. Liberty. Happiness.

Our group walked briskly down the long path, hardly talking, each carrying our own thoughts, until we arrived at Mr. Byrd's Town Car, cleared of brush the day before. So far — except for the boy by the road — our shoddy perimeter had held. Mr. Byrd opened the trunk, which was tidy and bare but for jumper cables. The faint smell of gasoline wafted up, turning my stomach. How would I manage to ride back there without getting sick, and with Devin beside me? Mr. Byrd placed the keys in Knox's hand. *Drive like you mean to get there,* he said.

Then Mr. Byrd called us into a huddle, his voice clarifying the most direct route, along with an alternate one. He ended by restating our mission: Get MaViolet's medication. See about the road, the neighborhood, town. Grab batteries if we could. Nonperishables. *Bring yourselves back to us,* Mr. Byrd concluded, kicking a slender fallen branch from the road. We pulled our heads apart.

Knox tugged me to one side. *Are you sure, Da'Naisha?*

Are you, I said, and then again, more softly: *Are you?*

Carol hugged Ira and kissed the single white hen he'd carried all the way down the hill; it lurched back, casting red-laced feathers. Devin dapped Elijah and Ezra, then they all wrapped their arms around one another. Knox hugged me and I burrowed my face into his chest, praying again like I'd prayed over MaViolet's bed two nights before. Let us live, I prayed. The sun reached us through gaps between the branches, dappling our limbs with light, setting a whole series of spiderwebs aglow — shining mandalas all through those woods around us that had been invisible a moment before. I prayed to something shapeless and not my own, to the murky future, bargaining wordlessly: Please let us make it back! Then I climbed into the trunk, fighting a

tremor that had returned to my limbs, trying to make my body small.

Devin climbed in behind me, smelling of
sweat and woodsmoke — waves of heat rolling off him as he folded himself around me.

Godspeed, Mr. Byrd said, laying an antique quilt over us, heavy and stinking of
mold.

The trunk clicked closed, and in that
sealed darkness, I could feel the engine
shiver to life. We began to move, slowly at
first, our tires churning leaves. The itch of
that old quilt against our skin and the gritty
sound of road beneath our bodies. From
the blackness, I imagined the bright world
passing: us rolling back beneath the light-
colored bridge, landing on the narrow route
that would deliver us back home.

Behind mine, Devin's body felt rigid. Felt
like he was trying to avoid touching me,
except in that tight space, he could not help
but touch me. I could feel his legs, his chest
damp with heat. He'd draped his right arm
over my hip, right where my bruise
throbbed. In that same hand, he held one
of his uncle's handguns, a pistol. Back in
grade school, Devin won this big award for
a student who excelled the most in history.
They gave it out at his fourth-grade gradua-
tion, a dim stage and all the girls in skirts

and blunt heels, and all the boys in borrowed ties, too long and tucked into their slacks. On the stage, they lifted a plaque into the light, promising that Devin's full name would soon be engraved at the end of the long column of names. Devin was tall even then, but on the stage that day, he'd hunched shyly, tilting his head as if to level his slightly crooked fade. Now we had Devin pegged as security. And he *had* defended us, that night back on First Street and at the welcome pavilion. Here he was again, defending us, defending me. But what else did he hope for?

We'll be there soon, I whispered, desperate to fill the dark.

Devin spoke almost at once. *Naisha, I already know.*

I was caught, literally, my legs tucked in, my arms pressed up against my chest. I squeezed my hands so hard my nails sank deep into my palms. *Know what,* I whispered.

He doesn't even know though, does he? Is it his or is it mine?

I could feel the car negotiating the narrow road, banking one way then the other — that series of S curves — and my stomach tightening with each turn. Had we passed beneath the white clapboard tavern or the black wood of the sawmill and general store? Devin knew I was pregnant. Despite my worry and hiding, he knew.

I didn't mean for this to happen, I said.

I could feel Devin tense with impatience, with anger, but he spoke gently. *You came to me,* he said.

Out of nowhere, we felt the car brake too quickly, and swallowed our words. Then we were speeding up again, turning so sharply our bodies slid to one side. My chest filled with an electric readiness, but there wasn't anywhere for that energy to go in that pent-up space. We were sailing up; then, jolting, we crashed to near stillness. A sound like a soft explosion.

A car door creaked open, footfalls, and I could feel Devin's arm tense fiercely on top of mine.

This is it, I thought. Even if Devin shoots whoever opens this trunk, even if he manages to do that . . . The ringing had filled my head again, still the sharp click of the trunk latch cut through.

I am not ready, I thought.

I want to finish college.

I want to have my first class full of eight-year-olds, watch them mark their desks with their names.

I want to see my grandma up and well.

Blinding light broke in and Devin had his gun ready, but it was Knox, just Knox, his face drained of color and all the angles gone slack. Knox yanked me out of the trunk and drew me to him. His body felt unfamiliar, as if it was surging with adrenaline and fear, or maybe mine did. Then Devin was out and up on his feet, the quilt on the ground beneath him.

What? Where — Devin stammered.

Knox pointed down the hill. *Oh shit! They're coming!*

We were partway up a driveway, crashed into a gate that had torqued but not given way, and someone was coming, though I could not see who. The Town Car's hood was crumpled, the blooming white of an airbag filling the passenger side. I ran around toward it. Still seated, Carol looked at me stunned. I heard a pop-pop sound.

Get down! Get behind the car, somebody said.

Someone shouted my name.

It was Knox.

It was Devin.

Knox ran to me, and together we pulled Carol out. The three of us crouched in the space between the hood and the broken gate, Knox's body slightly in front of Carol and me, his arms stretched back, as if to

257

shield us. Devin was still standing near the open trunk. The gun looked like a toy in his hand.

Stay down, Devin said.

That sound again, tinny, distinct. I saw leaves skitter.

Devin kept his gun lifted, his arm like an arrow. He held his body sideways as he walked into the space between. One step then another, closing the distance. He must've been shooting too, firing back. I heard a low grunt, then shouting that was not our shouting. When I craned my head up again, I saw two men in the woods below us, cloaked in spring camo, forest green and brown, that flash of blue pinned to them. One man was folded over, holding the meaty part of his thigh, like a bloody trophy. Had Devin shot him? Devin must have shot him because the other man had stopped shooting in order to drag the bent man out of view.

Devin! I shouted.

I was right behind him, grabbing his back arm, though he did not seem to feel my hands on him. He didn't look at me but instead took another shot. My tugging must've changed the arc of that final bullet, which seemed to reach nothing. Now the two men were lost in the trees, hiding or else hobbling back down to their vehicle below.

We gotta go, I said.

Devin turned back to us and took it all in. The ruined car, the gun in his hand. Carol's crimson face, and Knox standing halfway between, pale with disbelief. My fingers were still on Devin's skin, but I drew them back. Without more words, we moved all together, skirting the broken gate to reach the paved drive above it. Together, we ran up and away.

X.

The road was steep and winding. Its paved arm twisted one way then the other, lined in woods. We jogged and stumbled upward, halting when we lost our breath. Even in our harried state, Knox reached for my arm, begged me to say I was okay. All I could do was nod.

In a blurred voice, as if he were drunk, Knox recounted what had happened below. There'd been a pickup, he told us, abandoned in the middle of the road, just beyond the head of the driveway we were now ascending. Not a broken-down ambush like Lakshmi'd described — this time no one was visible, inside or out. Knox hoped the truck had simply run out of gas. But then, as they got closer, Knox had seen a man's head rise from the truck bed. Aiming a rifle. Shouting for Knox to stop.

But he didn't stop: Knox told us he *knew* he couldn't.

Instead he'd slowed, then sped up, and at the last second, veered left and barreled up the same driveway we were still stumbling along. But the man with the rifle had followed him. In fact, there had been two men. Maybe the men knew there was a gate. Knox had not. When he saw the gate, Knox had laid on the gas, hoping to burst through.

It's hard for a body to keep running upward. Carol's sandals clacked against the pavement, and Knox's breathing sounded harsh around his words. I lurched forward, my throat coated with fear, which tasted like smoke. My mouth filled with warm saliva and mucus until I had to bend over to try to spit it out, coughing, gagging. I wanted to throw up — to get that feeling out of me — but all I could do was retch.

Naisha, come on, Devin said.

I still couldn't look at him, now that *I* knew *he* knew — but in truth, I felt some kind of relief, that someone else knew everything.

We started again, walking fast.

Were those the same men — Knox started.

The blue, I said. *On First Street, those men wore blue armbands too.*

Our fear drove us forward, even as our lungs burned with effort, even as Carol turned to look back down the road. Knox tugged me by the wrist, his Adam's apple jumping as he swallowed. Devin still held that pistol close at his leg, as if ready to use it or else like he'd forgotten he held it. Of course, those men were blocking the road; it had been reckless to let myself believe otherwise. I'd wanted to believe they'd put away their weapons, scrubbed the smell of fuel from their hands, and used those cleaner hands to touch wives or lift their own children. That they'd soon use their reach for something useful, for restoration even. Because who on earth benefited from this rift?

Carol slowed, swaying in a patch of light, and we all used that moment to gulp in air. She had not said a word since we'd tugged her from the Town Car. I scanned her body for blood, for any sign of fracture. She looked uninjured, but her eyes were too dark, as if the brown centers had eaten the whites.

You shot that man, Carol said to Devin. *Now they are going to come and find us and shoot us.*

Devin looked down at his gun and tucked it hastily into his waistband, pulled his T-shirt over it, before looking back at Carol. *What did you expect me to do?* he said.

We began to walk again, passing a metal guardrail, a gully. Moving through luminescent globes of gnats swarming. The air filled with the ripe, singed scent of late spring.

Where does this road lead? Knox said.

I realized where we were as I said it: *We're on the drive to the orchard,* I answered.

We kept on, moving as fast as we were able, sweat rolling down on our backs. I was so thirsty, but we'd left our bag with water and a few supplies in the Town Car. I could hear dogs baying in the distance.

We've gotta be almost to the top by now, I said.

Finally, the woods began to open up, giving way to meadowland. The sun spotlit our heads, searing our scalps and setting a fiery edge to the unshorn grass. The hills rolled upward, lined in trellises with vines intertwined. Ahead and to our right, we soon saw a long gravel lot. Beyond that, apple trees lined up, a mottle of tattered blossoms and weatherworn leaves.

Wait — this road ends here, Devin said. *Where're we s'pose to go from here?*

The lot was empty except for a handful of

vehicles, spread apart. At the far end, we could see a set of barnlike structures, brick red, with picnic tables cascading down the slope behind them. When I'd worked at Monticello, tourists would drive to Jefferson's plantation after picking fruit at the orchard. Come fall they would have cradled pumpkins, bought jugs of cider, taken their kids on tractor rides.

We've gotta get out of the open, I said.

Crisscrossing the lot, we peered into car windows, pulling up locked latches, wondering if we might be able to coax one of those vehicles into motion. But where could we even get to from there? Everything on that hill — in the lot and below the fruit trees — was still except for us. As we moved across the gravel, we could see that the closest building had been badly damaged, the roof breached. Storm debris had collected in a break, like a massive bird's nest. Behind us, the road gaped — empty still, but for how long? I felt sure the men would rush into view at any moment. How hard would it be to get past our Town Car or the gate? Maybe we'd hear their pickup — more likely, they'd arrive with more men, more vehicles, more guns.

We could hide in one of these buildings, Knox said.

Devin plucked his T-shirt away from his body. *If we hide in there, what we going to do when they get here? I shot at them, remember?*

You did not shoot "at" them, Knox said. *You shot them — one of them.* Knox's voice was sober again, but distant, like when he was working out a difficult equation.

What the fuck y'all want me to do, Devin said. *Let them shoot you? Shoot us?*

I could tell Knox was still calculating, looking up at space above Devin, as if the answer was floating there. *When I saw those men,* Knox went on, *I knew I couldn't stop. Because you were in the trunk. If the trunk had been empty, they might have let us through —*

You think it's my fault, our fault, Devin said, palming his own chest, pointing at me.

Knox's eyes came back down, landing on Devin. *That's not what I mean,* he said.

Felt like Devin's body had been whipped into frantic motion, even though his feet were still planted. *Isn't it, though?*

Knox raised his palms in defense, like he had that first night before Devin punched the Jaunt. *Why do you hate me so much?*

Why you need everybody to love you? Devin said.

I'm not like them, Knox said, his face betraying some new sadness, or maybe the same old one that drew me to him at the start.

Do something, then, Devin said.

Knox let his hands fall. *What the fuck do you want me to do?*

Watching them go back and forth, my body grew so heavy — there was so much loss there, and not just mine. *I'm the one who insisted on coming,* I said, my voice overflowing with that loss. *We're fucked and I need you both to help figure this out. So quit fighting and put the blame on me, okay?*

Devin and Knox both went silent, choking back words, their dispute suspended. They might have gotten right back to it except that Carol interrupted. She'd walked out toward the edge of the gravel lot where the land sloped down. Now she stood visoring her eyes with her hand, peering northward toward town. *What is happening down there?* Carol said.

We moved alongside her to try to see what she was seeing.

Past the heads of the trees, a haze obscured our view, smoke funneling out from someplace that felt close to the road below us. A wildfire maybe, like the ones out on the West Coast, though the smoke seemed more localized. I tried to imagine the land below us as if I were looking down from high above. What was down there, besides woods, between us and the highway? Seemed like the smoke was rising from where the Blue Ridge Sanatorium was — a compound of crumbling buildings that had once, long ago, housed the city's white patients with tuberculosis, touting sunshine and fresh air. Later, it was used in other ways, and eventually it was purchased by the university, though it had been closed to the public for many years. I'd been to Blue Ridge precisely once, back in high school, invited to come along by a couple of white girls I knew from my honors classes. We'd met up with two SUVs full of football players, in the lot near the Saunders-Monticello Trail. Together we'd walked through pitch dark to scale the fence, the boys' backpacks heavy with beer. One of them knew the caretaker was gone that weekend — we would not get busted, he assured us. Even so, as we stood before those once-beautiful buildings — a grand residence hall boarded up all along its face, a chapel dripping with moss, the footballers already starting to build a small fire on the pavement — I hadn't felt safe there. I hadn't stayed.

More houses on fire, Carol said.

Knox said, *A bonfire, maybe.*

You think it's them, Devin said to me. *It's gotta be them, Naisha, right?*

I tugged at the gaping scoop at my collar. *Prob'ly,* I said.

My God — look at town, Devin said.

Through the bluish fan of smoke, we could see sets of faultless red rooftops — but then too, black footprints where some of the buildings by the lake should have been. Oily smoke fanning up from what looked like Belmont and an odd checkerboard of damage had been stamped across downtown and northward with charred remains between unmarred stretches. Near the university, the massive white tower of the hospital had been transformed to a blackened shell: my whole hometown, a patchwork of ruin.

Da'Naisha, Knox said.

When I turned to look at Knox, there were people behind him. Across the lot, a group of men stood where moments earlier there had been no sign of anyone. More bodies began to trickle out of the brick-red buildings in a thick braided line. Men, women, and children rounded that closest damaged barn, slowly revealing their numbers: maybe five times as many people as we had on our mountain. A trio of collies leapt barking into the space between.

What should we do? Carol said.

The orchard people trod toward us until their line was as far away from us as the length of three cars, maybe. It curved around our foursome like a giant horseshoe, or a fat rope tightening. Pink and tan faces tilted. Eyes squinted below sunhats and baseball caps. Hands lifted shovels, axes, hoes, with only the inner row of men carrying long rifles, which they kept pointed toward the ground. The things they carried, along with their numbers, suggested that they did not *want* to hurt us, but that they could.

We all raised our hands, even Devin. Devin's handgun remained tucked in the back of his waistband, but sweat had made his white T-shirt translucent as a veil. Please, please don't see Devin's gun, I thought.

One man dressed in denim and flannel stepped ahead of the group, moving halfway between them and us. He looked sinewy, his face gaunt and lined with age or wear. His head alone was bare — not covered like everyone else's. His hair, chestnut-colored and streaked in silver, funneled down the back of his neck. He almost looked like a hapless farmer except there was something flashing in his eyes. The collies, fur mottled in black and white, whined obediently at his feet.

Desperate times, the man said. Behind him, the orchard people nodded or cleared their throats. A few beat the ends of their tools against the gravel. *Up here, we don't invite trouble.*

Listen, Devin started, his body already arced with that restless urgency from earlier that I felt in my limbs too. *There were these zealots, down on the road, these crazy fuckers — they shot at us, chased us —*

The orchard man cut in. *Son, we are decent people.*

He looked at Devin, who was sweating, like we all were sweating, and then away.

Man, they were about to kill us, Devin said.

All I could think was, Devin, raise your hands back up — keep them up!

This one, the man said, gesturing at Devin, but looking at Knox, at Carol. At me, even. *Calm him down. Is he on something?* The man's voice was so steady that we knew better than to answer. Carol began to make a small sound, like a word caught in her throat.

Goddamn, Devin muttered, but he raised his arms high and stilled his body, until he looked like a statue of someone in perpetual surrender.

No, Knox said. *What he said is true. There were men, blocking the road. We don't know them. They shot at us. We think they're going to follow us here.*

The man looked Knox up and down. *We don't invite trouble,* he said.

Help us, Knox said. *We need to get away — we've got to get back . . .*

Knox's voice trailed off, and his light eyes drifted, as if he'd lost his aim and meant to find it in the hazy air. Where did he hope to get back to, precisely? Back to First Street, or to the university? Back to Washington State?

Monticello, I said.

My raised arms were trembling from the effort of demonstrating that I meant no harm. Around us, the orchard people coughed and twitched, shifting weight, as if our desperation had agitated their bodies. *Help us to get back to Monticello,* I said, willing my voice steady and appeasing, like I'd done so many times before. But my throat burned as if I'd been forced to swallow embers.

I could feel the orchard man weighing my request.

We've had some interesting visitors, he said, glancing back at the others, many of whom nodded. *I'm afraid helping people like you would most certainly be trouble.*

Like us, Devin said.

Leave on your own or we'll be forced to help you leave, the man said.

You should help us, Knox said. *You have to —*

Carol was still making that noise, a call held in.

The line of orchard people was already retreating, with only a handful of the men — the ones who held long rifles — remaining to watch us. We started for the driveway, our footfalls unsteady but hurried, our chests caved in. We'd put some distance between ourselves and the orchard men when Carol doubled back, dashing toward them, her sandals skimming gravel. We caught her well before she reached them, our hands hooked into her elbows, pulling her back. She shouted past the men, toward the backs of the heads of the orchard people, almost to the first barn.

Lorraine! Carol shouted, sounding shriller with each repetition. *Lorraine!* Carol knew or thought she knew one of the women. *I see you, Lorraine! Please make these people help us!*

But Lorraine, whoever she was, did not answer.

XI.

We knew it then, undeniably: There were white men gunning for us along the road to town. Still we were shocked to find a lone Black man, without any weapons, bound and waiting on our own mountain when we returned.

We'd made it back to Monticello by scrambling headlong into the mouth of unfamiliar woods, midway down the orchard's long paved drive. We'd clambered over ravines, up banks so steep our ankles throbbed. Legions of ticks lay in wait in tall grasses, crawling up our calves, trying to latch to skin before we brushed them off. There was, we knew, a sturdy boardwalk path that would have more comfortably delivered us that few miles back. But the easier path, like the road right below it, risked our being seen even more than the woods did. By the time we got back, we were dripping with sweat, our lungs raw-feeling, our bodies full of a dull, profound hunger.

When we staggered out of the woods near the welcome pavilion, our trio of guards — Lakshmi along with Gary and Ira — ran out to meet us. But they hardly took in our terrible adventure, why we were carless and sick with thirst. Instead they alerted us that there was another stranger at the house. Ira clutched Carol, and Gary brought us plastic bottles refilled with cistern water, his black-and-blue hair dripping as if he'd recently dunked it against the heat. Had we made it to town, to First Street, they asked. We told them we had not.

You should hurry, Lakshmi said. She'd found lipstick somewhere; her lips stood out, a deep rust color. *He's up at the house,* she said. *You should see for yourselves.*

When we came up on the backyard, no one was in sight. No one was working down in the gardens or playing up along the terraced side yard. Not one person was visible along the south terrace or in the reconstructed shelters of Mulberry Row. A blistering wind pushed at my body, and I felt light, like I might be swept up into the billowy architecture of the clouds. They rushed over our heads, throwing peculiar shadows to the ground.

Carol and Ira took off toward their white textile workshop above the garden, but Knox and Devin followed me. The three of us passed swiftly through the greenhouse room and Jefferson's crowded cabinet. When we reached MaViolet's bedchamber, Ms. Edith was there, sitting tall in her dedicated chair near the window, hands busy with work at her lap. We blundered in and she released her squinting focus, addressing us as children. *Y'all get her medication? Our houses still standing?*

I shook my head, kissed MaViolet's cheek. It felt like she'd gone down even in the few hours since I'd looked at her early that morning. Her eyes were still closed, but her face held that new grim expression, a twisting I wanted desperately to see eased. The room stank of bodies, of wood ash, though maybe that funk emanated from our skin: Devin's and Knox's and mine. Behind me, Devin asked where this stranger was, and Ms. Edith directed us out front with an arched finger, her sewing needle pinched between her teeth.

Out front beyond the east porch, toward the gatepost of the twin linden trees, everybody else had gathered. Right away, I could see the stranger too, his head low. He was seated, I realized as I got closer. He'd been tied by his wrists and ankles to the black-painted chair that held him. His T-shirt and long pants were largely in tatters and when I got right up on him, I saw that his feet were bare. What I thought right away was, Who are *we* to do this to anybody? Who have we become? Only later did I realize our mistake: letting him see how few we were.

Y'all made it back! Ezra shouted, and the twins surrounded Devin in their arms.

Greetings rose from the small congregation, a brief but palpable expression of relief to see us again. But their hugs for us were like shallow breaths. Folks used the rest of the air in their lungs to question us about town, then to tell us about the bound man, as we stood to one far side of the path so that he might not overhear.

How was our place?

Daddy's grave, the yellow house?

Folks out around the hood?

They blocked the road — I worried they would.

This man — I know! He walked right up here, no shoes on his feet. Keeps saying the same damn thing!

They told us that the stranger had nearly made it to the east porch, not long after we'd left that morning. He'd crept up through the northwest woods, avoiding the welcome pavilion altogether. KJ, who'd been playing hide-and-seek, counting to one hundred on the steps, head down but peeking, had seen the man first. When KJ got to shouting, Mama Yahya came running, jiggling the baby. Mr. Byrd arrived right away,

275

but he'd left his shotgun inside. They all told us that the stranger had kept coming, his arms loose and swinging. He'd kept coming, even after Yamileth got Mr. Byrd's shotgun. Even after Mr. Byrd raised that gun, demanding that the man stand down. Even after Elijah barreled over, his voice as assured as his body was imposing. The stranger's heedlessness had kicked up a wide panic that we could still feel in the air around us, all those hours later.

In the end, the twins, working together, had tackled the stranger to the ground, because he would not stop, but no one had quite been able to shoot him, this wild-eyed Black man approaching with empty hands.

My sons and I, we tied him up, Mr. Flores said. *He was not having any weapons on his body.*

Mr. Byrd took stock of the three of us there who'd tried and failed to get to town. *You all ought to hear what he's been saying. Must have said the same thing a hundred times.*

Our group turned back, encircling the barefoot man.

He was raw-boned, deep-complected like me, and filthy. He looked to be in his thirties, maybe, and he wore a blue armband like the white men who'd set fires, except

276

this Black man's banner had fallen from his emaciated biceps so that it circled his wrist like a cuff. Up close, I could see it was an upside-down flag of Virginia.

Knox studied the man's profile from one side.

Devin crouched to eye level.

I moved closer to him. *What do you want?* I said.

Up close, the man smelled like sweat and urine and feces. His bare feet were and laced with bloody scrapes and gashes. I was so thirsty from our long walk, but I held my water bottle to the man's cracked mouth. He gulped greedily until I took it away.

Tell them like you been telling us, Mr. Byrd said.

The strange man shook against his bindings. He lifted his head, stretching his mouth wide open, before he began. When he spoke, he sounded stilted, his diction way too tight.

It is my privilege to be allowed to speak for the True Men, the Patriots, the man said. *They say, We are chosen to redeem the great state of Virginia from darkness. They say, We pledge to do what must be done, to restore our Legacy! Our Monuments! Ourselves!* As the man spoke, it became clear he was reciting something, the slanted way each word fell into the next. *They move — we move — with swiftness, with righteousness in this moment of chaos! We must not fail lest this commonwealth fail, lest America fail . . .*

I listened without speaking, trying to take it all in, even as my tongue twitched in my mouth. I was braced to interject, to correct or argue, but it was so much: his degraded appearance, his erring elocution, the audacity of the words themselves.

He crazy, right? Ezra said.

The man kept speaking, stumbling over his *we*'s and *they*'s then doubling back to lay them straight. Toward the end of his oration, he attempted to stand, forgetting — I guess — that he was tied down to something. Seemed like he had rehearsed that speech many times and always on his feet.

Nonetheless his voice rose along with his gaze. *You people are trespassing!* he shouted, spittle flying, his voice pitching toward a crescendo. *You people owe an unpayable debt! You owe for your Welfare, your Public Housing, your Petty Crimes. You owe for your children who pollute our public pools and classrooms. You people owe us this Great House, this Great Man, both of which are ours!*

I thought of that young white woman, the one who'd been murdered by the man in a car, but who'd also died of a ravaged heart.

I thought of various groups ringed around Jefferson's statue at the university or encircling the old monument that loomed above a public park in town. For me, the menace from those relics came when I learned more about the circumstances of their installation. My anxiety grew as I watched the men stomp and chant so fearsomely around them. They seemed to want to remember in glory a thing my family hoped America would never forget. As the strange man spoke, I was thrown back, yet again, to the night I'd peered out through MaViolet's blinds. That windowless white van parked across the way, the teen spouting blood who'd been thrown bucking into it. What had they done to that boy? Had this lost man in front of us been stolen from some neighborhood like ours? The man looked up at the roof of the house, toward the crooked weathervane; there was something dead at the center of his eyes, where the light should have been, where we should have seen ourselves reflected.

Surrender the House! His voice rang out. *Surrender the House within forty-eight hours or else it shall be liberated!*

The man slumped forward, but he could fall only so far because of the way we'd bound him. I held my water to his lips again, even though I despised him. I could hardly stand to look at him after hearing his dark declaration: what the men below thought of us, what they hoped to do. They thought *we* owed *them*. They believed their security depended on making sure we never felt safe, not even in our own bodies. Their claims, along with their brutal means, trampled over the simple fact of my family: MaViolet and Momma and me. I felt it then, deep in my belly and maybe for the first time, that knotted tie to Monticello like a rope or a bridge. My bond by blood *and* water — as master and slave. My ancestors had conceived of this house and bloodied their hands to build and maintain it.

I wanted to shake the barefoot man like I'd shaken that boy on the road in the dark. Had that boy told the men about us? Is that how they knew we were living up here, Black and armed and afraid? And had that even been the same boy or had my reckless fury been the seed of some random child's budding hate? Either way, I upended my water bottle. The man drank savagely, water gushing down his face.

Maybe it was because of the water or because I am a young woman that he looked at me like he recognized me. Face shadowed with wild sorrow, he mumbled something, his voice skittish at first, a voice unsure of where to go. *They got my girls,* the man said, tears streaming and wrestling again against our ropes. *They got my girls — they not but seven and thirteen. Now please let me go back.*

After we let the strange man leave, tying strips of cloth around his feet, like bandages and shoes all at once, and escorting him into the woods he'd come from, I hurried back to check on MaViolet. I was startled to find her awake, lucid. Ms. Edith was still by her bed, rocking and singing a hymn Ma-Violet loved. Her mouth hung slightly parted and her eyes seemed to have gone milky. Her gaze roamed up and around before landing on my face.

Ma, I said. I lifted her hand in mine.

She looked hard at me, as if she could see *through* me. Her jaw began to work, the muscles drawing in like she was struggling to wake her mouth up, but her tongue stayed sunk, and no words came out.

I parted my own lips, still cracked with thirst, intending to tell her all of it. About the barefoot man and the orchard people. About the child on the road whom I'd beaten and run off. I meant to tell her about my body's unfolding toward motherhood —

how astonishing it was, how absurd it was — but I was terrified.

Instead I sang a few lines of that old hymn Ms. Edith was singing, my voice going slick against the back of my throat.

Precious lord, take my hand,
Lead me on, let me stand,
I am tired, I am weak, I am worn.

I could not leave her just then, so I asked Knox to gather everybody, even the children. I asked him to call them into this house where our muddy footprints marked the parquet flooring. Where oil from our fingers lacquered brassy key hooks and collected on the strings of bygone instruments we couldn't quite name but managed to pluck an odd tune from. Where the heat of our bodies, along with our sweat, left deep impressions on high beds and sunken chair cushions.

Bring them in here, I said.

I figured, if we met in Jefferson's cabinet, that office-like space between the bedchamber and his personal library, then at least I could look over my shoulder at Ma-Violet, awake and with us. *Those men are coming for us,* I whispered to her. *They're practically here.*

Truth is, I'd already known they were coming, even before the barefoot man told us. Even before the unraveling: those old flags brandished and baiting fliers flung. I knew it as a girl, when they killed that young woman, then blamed her own body. It was a hitch deep in my lungs, reminding me not to breathe too easy. I inherited my knowing from Momma, and from MaViolet before her: I was born knowing.

Hold on, MaVi, I said as I waited for folks to arrive. I was standing at her bedside, still clinging to her hand. I was thinking it had been a terrible mistake to drag her up here, and for what? And after all she had sacrificed for me. Getting me through high school after Momma passed and our spirits were battered. Urging me ever forward and toward that fancy university — *And why not you, Grandbaby,* she'd said. MaViolet had insisted we keep on striving, keep on hoping, even through our infinite grief.

Body by body, folks brought themselves into the cabinet room and adjacent library, their voices low as if at a wake. Their voices full of fear because of our failed expedition and all the barefoot man had said. Mr. Byrd spoke in a low voice to MaViolet, but her eyes were blinking closed again. To fit, folks wove their bodies around Thomas Jefferson's things: his desk and famed handwriting machine, which allowed two pens to move in tandem, making easy twins for his letters, for posterity. His tables and globes. The students wedged themselves against window ledges, mindful of a wooden bureau that held an ivory bust. Ira and Carol squeezed in along a sofa the color of KJ's suitcase, with Yamileth teetering at one edge, her slim face angled up at me. The Yahyas treaded between a surveying tool and an angled telescope, most everything brassy or cherry brown, not unlike that small exhibit at the museum below that the children had loosed.

Devin came in last, just after KJ and the twins and Georgie, but from the opposite direction. He must have passed through our glass-faced greenhouse, stepping over the pallet where Knox and I had slept side by side each night.

Once everyone was there, Knox made his way back to me. Hands on my back, he hastened me to turn and face them.

We have to decide, I said, my voice edged in frailty or else jurisdiction. *Right now,* I said. *There's no more time.*

It was with that sense of urgency that folks recounted the details of the day. Each small story linking into our larger one, until the whole of it belonged to all of us. Carol spoke about the armed men in the pickup and Knox described how the orchard people had sent us away. Mr. Byrd and Elijah, along with KJ, retold the story of the barefoot man approaching. Together, in bursts, we worked to pick apart and weigh his grisly message.

So now they snatching up and holding Black people, Ezra said.

Devin laid a hand on Ezra's shoulder, to calm or comfort him, but making contact with Ezra's exasperation only riled Devin's own body back up. *What you think they doing to that dude's children?* Devin said.

Papa Yahya ran a hand over his hair, which, when brushed back, held undulating ripples. Beside him, his son tugged at his elbow. *His feet,* Jobari exclaimed. *Did you see his feet, Papa? Will our feet be like his?*

I told everybody about the great plume of smoke we'd seen, how we thought the men might be gathering or camping at the old sanatorium, near the highway. I tried to describe what we'd seen of town: the fire-ravaged buildings and patchy broad damage, how it looked more widespread than what those men could do on their own. What else had happened down there? What was going to happen? When I described the ruin of our hometown, I thought I felt Ma-Violet's gaze, bright and hot, on the back of my head.

Forty-eight hours, Mr. Byrd said.

Fresh anger, deep anguish, and a renewed sense of terror spread through the room, evidenced by new tics in the composition of our faces, by wringing hands and rocking feet. KJ backed into a grandfather clock, taller than his body, hanging against a library wall. *Where's my bag at,* he called to the Yahya children. *For real, did y'all move it, I haven't seen it in days.*

Mr. Flores said something softly, in Spanish. His older son, Edward, echoed him in faultless English, in a cadence native to our country, our state, our town, our street: a kind of prayer.

Below me, Yamileth tugged at my ragged hem, her dark hair streaming around her skinny teenage face. *We cannot let them win,* she said, her voice full of nerve and gravel. I felt just the same, but despairing too. They had all those people, all those vehicles and weapons. How could we win against their righteous rage?

We murmured to ourselves and to each other, trying to work out that impossible equation, to make it come out in our favor. The sun was already starting to sink, like it always sinks, the room slowly filling with shadows.

There's no more time, I said again.

We have to leave, Carol said, standing up from the low green sofa and taking a small stumbling step. *We'll take what we can, and we'll just — leave, like before. We can drive the other way, away from town. We can walk, even. We can find some other town. We can camp in a field —*

I tried to move forward too, but my hip hit the jutting edge of the revolving stand to my right, recalling that old bruise, a feverish throb. I wanted to crawl back into bed with MaViolet, or to run. I was fast, I knew that now: I could be fast. But I could feel Ma-Violet behind me, twisting against those gritty bedsheets. In front of me, Jobari and Imani clung to Mama Yahya's legs as if they were much younger. Lakshmi whispered something to LaToya, and I thought about Lakshmi's long, frightening drive to her parents' cul-de-sac and the old flag, hidden there. I could feel, as if encased in darkness, that turn we took too quickly, our rushed ascent, only to crash to a halt at the gate. The loose sound of Carol's sandals against gravel and the moan that rose in me when I saw the stranger's desecrated feet. Felt I could hear dogs barking in the distance.

We've got to stay together, I said. *We've got to protect one another.*

Ms. Edith was sitting in her chair in the bedchamber, looking through MaViolet's tunnel of a bed at me. *His will,* she said. *On earth as it is in heaven.*

Ms. Edith, I knew, had marched with church groups on the streets of Washington, DC, back in the day. And in town, she'd hectored many a city official to serve *our* neighborhood too, rallying folks to speak up, to stand up for themselves. She'd come regularly to sit with MaViolet well before the unraveling and deep into it, bringing fresh food and gossip. I knew Ms. Edith as a person who prayed through action, with her raised voice and lifted hands. Even so, when Ms. Edith said "His will" I felt like we might as well throw our hands up and follow the path past Jefferson's graveyard all the way back down beyond the welcome pavilion. File through the parking lot to where they'd found the stray bones of slaves — unadorned, unnamed — and lie on that rough uneven ground.

I could almost see us there.

We should fight, I thought, but I held my tongue. I must have muttered something, though, since everybody turned toward me again, each member of this new and chosen family of mine. Why is it we love what we love? I felt such love at that moment, for every soul in that space, because they were like me and different. Because we'd become a part of one another. I loved Knox, who had his hands on my shoulders as if to buffer me, lowering his sad and serious eyes. I loved the Yahyas in their bright colors. And LaToya, her hair half braided, half free, as she turned to look out the window; Ezra and Elijah too, like one side of a coin and the other. And Devin — I loved Devin, even if that love complicated everything. I loved all the children, coughing and playing, and Ms. Edith, out there in the wild rows. Even the rabbits' twitching faces, the birds claiming blackberries. I swear I loved the rich and loamy earth and the trees, especially the trees. Because we are all part of one another and sacred together.

We'll fight, I said, my voice unsteady. When I looked up my eyes caught on Devin, his back against books, locs tumbling around his face.

Way I see it, Devin said, *we just need to defend the top of this hill. Beat them down bad enough that they move on to the next one. Make them feel like this little bit here is ours.*

Maybe we can fool them, LaToya said.

Make them think we are without mercy, that we have lost our hearts, Mr. Flores said.

Maybe we could spook them, make them think we haunts, Ms. Edith said.

We could build some sort of barriers around the house, Ira said.

We know this house well, the lay of the land here, Mr. Byrd said.

Maybe we can hold them off — long enough for things to come back. That was Knox.

We fight! I said, my voice full of fury, full of hope.

We fight! everybody answered.

XII.

We worked deep into the darkness, planning then preparing, setting up a second guard post along the eastern border. I held the ladder for Mr. Byrd as he climbed up to wind the great clock above the main door in the entrance hall. Had I noticed its second face, he asked, on the front of the building? Did I know that, when wound, that clock triggered an hourly gong that could be heard down in the valley below? When I saw those hands set back into motion, I understood we were no longer hiding. Time had started up again.

When I finally had a moment to rest, I knew I'd never be able to sleep. Every creak in the house sounded like a warning, and when I squeezed my eyes closed, I felt filmy, weightless. I floated so high that I could see our whole town shimmering below me. From that great height, among the smoldering remains, I could see dark bands of men gathered, throwing old wood in to feed a fire: window frames jutting nails, floorboards slick with lichen. I could see the orchard people, hats resting on their chests, dreaming beneath the barn's breached roof, a bordered view of stars. I could see the barefoot man's dark-skinned daughters wrenching against the ways they'd been bound. I could hear the echo of sadness in Devin's voice, from all those hours earlier. *You came to me,* he'd said.

I must have slept some.

I woke to the clamor of the great clock, its vibration moving through my body, so that I bolted upright in a blackened room. I could make out Knox's sleeping form on our shared pallet. He must have come to bed sometime after I had. Now he rolled over, throwing his arm across my lap. At once, I remembered all that hung so heavily over us. I got up as quietly as I could, making my way across our small room, past the maze of tables and chairs in Jefferson's chambers, my eyes struggling to adjust to the dark. As they did, MaViolet's sleeping face emerged, her eyes pinched closed, her mouth unnaturally twisted. Ms. Edith was asleep in the chair by her bedside; she opened her eyes, then closed them again when she saw that it was me.

I had to go somewhere, but where to? I made my way through the parlor, toward the west porch. The night air felt dry and hot on my skin.

I crossed the pebbled path — my bare feet shifting stones — and crept onto the lawn, to try to catch some kind of breeze. The Flores family's tents remained huddled in a half circle way back near the tree line. The waning moon had withered, and dense clouds had rolled in, leaving the sky a tarry black. It felt so dark out, I could hardly remember streetlights. It seemed strange how much I'd counted on artificial light before — the blue aura of a TV in a neighbor's window, the far-off beams of headlights, revealing the edges of things. How I'd loved that easy, lavish light, hardly recognizing the ruin in its excess. I moved out into the grass, longing to see the full shining moon again.

I was almost to the small muddy fishpond when I sensed a gathering in the deep dark in front of me. I froze, listening, my heart drumming up in my ears. I took one step, then another, hardly registering the scratchy grass, the itch of insects at my ankles. I stretched my arms out into the space as if to touch plushness, a tawny pelt or the knobbed grace of antlers. But my quiet commotion scared them off: I heard their hooves scatter.

I was alone again.

I took a few more steps, and there, at the far end of the south terrace, was another shadow — a person standing near the massive trunks of the willow oaks. As I moved closer, I knew it was Devin, his familiar silhouette cut from blackness. There are oval-framed portraits along a wall of Jefferson's library, black profiles of significant people Jefferson knew. Devin is one of my significant people. When I saw Devin, I felt relief and something more.

It's my fault, I said right away when he looked up at me, as if we were picking up from those cramped moments in the trunk, before he'd raised a gun again in our defense. Devin did not seem surprised to see me — he was fidgeting with something, his Zippo lighter. Closing, it made a clicking sound. *And you're right,* I went on. *I did come to you.*

I thought he'd say, Fine, and tell me to go

back to my little college man, but he did not say anything. So I tried to answer his question from earlier, about being pregnant. I told him the truth: that I wasn't sure if the baby belonged to him or to Knox, or if it was even a *she*. When I told him this, I wanted to be able to hope for her.

Why did you come to me though? Devin said.

I scratched at my elbow, a new dry itch. *I already said it was my fault,* I told him.

Devin produced a cigarette from behind his ear and rolled the fragile white column between his fingers. *Why did you come around messing with me if you love him?*

Thing is, it had only ever been the two of them. First Devin. Then I'd waited a long, long time. Then Knox.

And just that one time, Devin again.

Remember that day, Naisha, he said, leaning against the rough broad trunk of the tree behind him. *How I said, it was something, what you'd done — building yourself up and still showing up in the neighborhood? It felt good, you coming to me, even if I knew you wouldn't stay.*

There's no going back now, I said.

Could be, could be not, Devin said. *Either*

way, it's something, what you did: bringing us here.

Devin lit his cigarette with the Zippo's steady flame. I hadn't seen him smoke since that very first night, but now the smell of menthol filled the air between us. The glow made me able to see him more clearly, the scruff on his cheeks, his otherwise smooth brown skin, his eyelashes casting long shadows.

Last one, he said, then like it was nothing, he placed the Zippo in my hands.

Here's the thing, Devin said, his voice wavering like it used to, way back. *It doesn't even matter why — not anymore. What matters now is the future, baby girl's future. Promise you won't come to me anymore. You and me are history. People like us, we do what we've got to do. What I'm asking you to do is go and tell him she's his and make him believe it. Because, the way I see it now, she got more of a chance with him as her daddy. Tell him, and please, please don't come around anymore.*

I started to say something, to argue with him maybe. I wanted to say something to lift him up, and myself with him, but no words formed between my teeth and tongue. Devin flicked his last cigarette down and stubbed it out beneath his boot tread. He

295

turned himself away from me so assuredly I knew he would not turn back. He walked to his far-flung room at the end of the terrace, leaving me alone and holding that small metal thing. Then I walked back to my room, to where Knox lay sleeping.

XIII.

Yesterday we started early, as if we'd never stopped. Almost twenty-four hours had passed since the barefoot stranger had arrived and shared the armed men's intentions. We'd have one more full day to prepare, if what he said held true. We'd gone back and forth about it, whether the stranger's stated timeline was a ruse. Maybe those men were on their way already. Or maybe they delivered a baseless threat to us in the hopes of scaring us off. There was no way to know for sure.

All day long we kept at it, between the hourly clanging of the newly wound clock, determining the best shooters among us, locating the most defensible lookouts. We divided our meager stash of weapons and ammunition, and chose evenly matched groups, like picking teams in grade school, each with a home base, a walkie, and a view in one of the cardinal directions, like Jefferson's weathervane. Mr. Byrd and some of the others sharpened bits of metal, to mark a spiky perimeter below Mulberry Row. The SCFP students handed out Mace and face masks. It no longer felt safe to send an envoy up to Montalto mountain, but Devin and the twins skidded up on the slant roof to look down to try to see what was happening below.

As I moved along the south terrace toward our greenhouse room, I couldn't help but notice how we'd transformed, yet again. In those intervening hours, everybody had bejeweled themselves with objects from the house. Carol and Ira were collecting food from the garden, but they sipped, every so often, from a pair of tarnished Jeffersonian goblets. The Flores men were dragging logs to make a blind along Mulberry Row, with Mr. Flores wearing a pair of binoculars, brassy and hanging from a thin leather string down his back. Georgie was splitting wood with Papa Yahya, who'd paired his cargo shorts with a billowy "Jefferson Everyday Shirt" I'd seen earlier in the giftshop. LaToya, who worked alongside Lakshmi and the other students as they painted a large banner, wore a tiny cowrie necklace on a chain at the hollow of her throat. Even Mr. Byrd's belt, which held up his newly sagging khakis, looked suspiciously like a period piece. I heard Ms. Edith pause in the side yard to speak to him in passing. *These daylilies,* she said. *Look at them, coming right on up. I suppose they won't show their orange faces for a few weeks yet —*

I paused just inside our giant window. I was still looking out at all of it when Knox came up behind me, placing his hand on the nape of my neck. All morning we'd been so terribly busy, with Knox running in one direction and me in the other, and both of us checking on MaViolet in between. Both of us doing everything we could think of, even if it did not feel like nearly enough. In addition to the sharpened metal, we'd run lines of wire between trees in places, to trip the men or bite at their shins if they came running up in darkness. We'd moved our food stores and water toward the center of the house. The kids dug a pit near the east walk and covered it with a sheet and leaves.

What else? Knox said, polishing his glasses with the edge of his shirt. My mind was racing; I threw out one variable after another.

What about the children?

We have them falling back to Mama Yahya, in the all-weather pass, he answered.

What about if they try to wait us out? I said.

Knox reminded me that the Flores brothers had set up those blinds so that they could pick men off. Shoot them. Discourage them. *We've got water,* Knox said. *If they wait, we wait.* Knox slid his frames back onto his face, where they'd listed to one side. *What about your grandma?* Knox said.

We'd been doing our best to make Ma-Violet comfortable, but she hadn't spoken or even taken water in more than a day. Her bed smelled of urine, and when I'd last tried to wash her, with a basin and rag, I could see sores up along her body even though we'd tried to turn her. Each breath left her chest curved like a question, one that might not be answered. At least she'd go in a bed, I told myself, trying to feel some kind of relief, but not feeling it. By her bedside, folks had begun to leave vases or cups spilling with blooms: foxglove, lilac, sweet William. A handful of faded tulips. What did it mean, her being here, I wondered — what did it matter?

What about us, Knox said, turning me to face him. *Are we okay, Da'Naisha? Do you still love me — do you still want me?*

Do you want me? I said, overlapping his words, feeling foolish and vulnerable and like the liar I was and still am. He took his glasses off again and sat them on the desk, so that his face shone, naked, open. He extended his arm, and I stepped close to his body, because I wanted to. He brought his arms carefully up and around me, and each place he chose to touch me felt polished. His fingers grazed my neck, his thumb stroked the bone at my collar. His chin nested against my part. *More now,* he said into the cushion of my hair. *I want you more now. I love you more.*

I'm pregnant, I said into his chest.

What, he said, cradling my shoulders and rocking me back so that he could see my face.

I'm pregnant, I said again.

Knox's face did a slow-motion time-lapse, from shock, to joy, to panic, then back to that joy, his hands large and trembling at either side of my face. He brought his mouth to my mouth, smiling, weeping, his hands never leaving me. He kept on kissing me, moving me back with those attentive hands, until I felt a wall behind my body. Until his whole body found mine, like mine was an extension of his, a feeling of pleasure so startling it almost brought the world back. *Oh God,* he said, like swearing, like praying. I may have echoed him. *God,* we whimpered. *God,* we cried.

XIV.

It's quiet now, almost sunrise again. As I write, I imagine men gathering below us, somewhere beyond our stone-covered bridge. The walkie on the chair ticks softly, and even though the signal has not yet come through, those men are coming. I know the way ghosts know, the way mothers do.

Yesterday afternoon, I couldn't help but notice how, amid frantic preparations, folks had found small ways to take care of themselves and one another. Ezra had brought up armfuls of fresh T-shirts from the gift shop, and LaToya and Gary helped him to pass them out to everybody. And Georgie, along with Carol, cleaned the first floor of the house, wiping dust from everything. Ira played a game of chess with KJ, the boy's sunken chest puffed up with pride. Mama Yahya came out of the parlor beaming, her children's hair gleaming in fresh braids or twists, along with Yamileth's. Ms. Edith and Lakshmi garnered help to cook a humble supper: saved eggs scrambled and cooked over a fire, with spring onions and thyme, chunks of potato dug right from the ground. Wild greens, cherries even, pitted and sweet. We hadn't eaten hot food since our attempt to go to town, and it felt like a feast, that meal we ate all together — even though our hearts trembled, our bodies were hungry still. Mr. Byrd brought out a crate of dusty bottles of wine, from some hidden place, and we ate and drank, bringing food down and trading off on the lower shift, so everyone could be a part of our fleeting celebration, because we all understood what was coming for us.

Earlier, I'd asked Mama Yahya if she might do something with my hair too. She'd had me lean my body back over a basin, in the lower yard, and ladled warm water over my head. Her fingers deftly raked my scalp, and afterward, sitting on the ground between her feet, I felt almost new. She'd set a straight part, combing my hair back and securing it into two tight knots at the nape of my neck. Before I got up, she folded a strip of fabric for me, wrapped it around the perimeter of my head, so that I was crowned in color.

I ate along with everybody, smiling despite the dread, laughing because sometimes you've got to laugh just to breathe. I could feel Knox looking at me with his new knowing: this vessel I am. At one point, Mama Yahya handed me her baby, her boy. He was heavy in my arms, his skin so delicate; he smelled of the lavender water she bathed him in. His weight on my lap felt like a kind of correction — like soil falling back into a hole, rich and newly full of air.

I ate; then I went to check on MaViolet once again.

I went to her hoping she'd be awake, that she might even take a bite of food in her mouth and taste how good it was. When I arrived, her body was still in that bed, but my grandmother Violet was gone. When I saw her, I thought of that time right after those early devastating storms. Police cars had lined up along First Street, lights pulsing blue and red in MaViolet's window. At first, people thought they'd been sent to help, to shuttle folks to shelters, or bring supplies, things needed since the power had been out. I knew that the police had been charged to help elsewhere in those weeks before they'd disbanded; they'd helped at the university. But that day, on MaViolet's street, a line of officers in helmets and shields stood facing the houses but not looking at the people inside, as if they'd been commanded not to see. For a period of about twelve hours, shifts of officers would not let anyone in or out. Not even for medication. Not even to get food or water. It pained her, she'd told me when I went to see her, to be an old lady and still the source of so much blame and fear that her own hometown would direct its resources against her. Now MaViolet lay there in her high bed, eyes silvery and flecked with yellow like mercury glass. And me, her last living relation. I put my hand on top of her hand and told her, finally, that I was pregnant. I told her I was determined to win some kind of way. I told her I would name my baby Violet, after her.

Then I stumbled out to the lawn to tell Knox, to tell everybody. They must have known from my expression. I collapsed to my knees and I could feel them, all around me. Somebody grasped my hand so hard I felt sharp nails digging, pain cutting through numbness, reminding me to take a breath. I could hear sobbing, mine or everybody else's, until our shared anguish was almost a song.

Back inside, Ms. Edith brought me a basin of warm water. I struggled to undress my grandma, to wipe down her body then pull her housecoat back up around her. It was Georgie who brought a bolt of faded fabric, fringed crimson, carrying it across his arms.

The sun was already falling when we buried my MaViolet, her body wrapped inside those curtains. We buried her alongside the pale path, the earth broken open, our shovels chipping through the tangle of roots. We lowered her body right into the ground, along with a square of Mama Yahya's precious fabric, halfway between Jefferson's gated graveyard and the slave cemetery below.

XV.

Some hours ago, Knox woke me on our pallet by the greenhouse windows. I felt his eyes on me even before he said my name into the dark.

Naisha, he said. *I don't know what I was thinking, but we are so fucked, honey. We just don't have enough,* he said. *Not enough people, or weapons, or anything. Those men are going to plow right through us.*

I wanted to say, I know already. But by then, it was so hard to swallow, to form words. I managed a couple. *We're here.*

Nineteen days, we've been here on top of this little mountain. Nineteen days, exploring dusty cellars and bright side rooms, slashing ribbons and touching everything: ours. Even the faulty map of Africa, even the crimson French curtains. We've wandered down the all-weather pass and roamed the unfettered grounds. We've huddled in the rebuilt slave cabin and imagined the searing heat of the iron house. Nineteen days feeling like nineteen years, and this morning, I can feel the men assembling below us in the quickening dark. Soon they will roar up past the trees and through the garden, trampling collards — there's no time left. I can almost hear them now.

Please know we fought with all we had — we fought to win. We fought with our bullets and bare knuckles, our bullhorns and Mace, our skepticism and our faith. I've collected everybody's names, along with the dates of our births and MaViolet's dying day. I'm placing these pages inside Thomas Jefferson's book, *Notes on the State of Virginia,* tucked between his accounting of the widths of our rivers, the heights of our mountains, his limits and his hope. I'll press that book back onto the shelf in the docents' library, this room where my grandmother's image hangs. Looking at her picture now, MaViolet looks stately, resplendent even. Maybe someday, someone will find our names, among books or ashes, and know that we were here, that we mattered too.

I don't know what will happen. I don't know what's happening elsewhere, outside of our town, our state. I only know I will not let them take this body of mine. I only know this fight will cost them something too. Mr. Byrd helped me to prepare the bottles, half full of gasoline with rags wagging out — I've got Devin's Zippo in my pocket, if it comes to that. They might well overtake us, but they will not win this house — not whole. If our bodies are found here, I hope we are buried between the two graveyards, so that we can stay together at least. Buried or not, we'll watch over all that happens here, forever and ever, along with all the others who've lived and dreamed and died here. Let our bodies fill the space between old and new, until all of it is indistinguishable, until all that remains is one great glow of souls lighting the way back home.

ACKNOWLEDGMENTS

This debut would not have been possible without the tireless support and fierce smarts of my fabulous agent, Meredith Kaffel Simonoff, as well as the immense care and enthusiasm of my generous editors, Retha Powers, Barbara Jones, and Kate Harvey. You all are amazing!

Thank you to the wonderful folks at DeFiore and Company, including Adam Schear, Colin Farstad, Emma Haviland-Blunk, Jacey Mitziga, Linda Kaplan, and Parik Kostan; at Henry Holt, including Allison Carney, Amy Einhorn, Caitlin O'Shaughnessy, Catryn Silbersack, Christopher Sergio, Gabriel Guma, Janel Brown, Jason Liebman, Jaya Miceli, Jolanta Benal, Maggie Richards, Maia Sacca-Schaeffer, Marinda Valenti, Nicolette Seeback, Patricia Eisemann, Rima Weinberg, Ruby Rose Lee, Sarah Crichton, and Vincent Stanley; and everyone at Harvill Secker and Vintage who supported this book.

With warmth and gratitude to Brooke Ehrlich and her team at Anonymous Content, including Becca Rodriguez and Jessica Calagione; everybody at the Chernin Group, particularly Peter Chernin, Jenno Topping, Kaitlin Dahill, and Christina Porter; as well as the fine folks at Netflix.

Thank you to the incomparable Roxane Gay, whose early story shout-out for "Control Negro" was the seed of this collection. Thank you to everybody at Best American Short Stories, especially Heidi Pitlor and Naomi Gibbs of HMH.

Thank you to the book people who championed my writing before this collection, in particular Jaimee Garbacik and Mackenzie Brady Watson. Also Rob McQuilkin. With gratitude to all of the authors who supported the launch of this debut or were willing to take an anxious call, even if you hardly knew me, like Nana Kwame Adjei-Brenyah. Thank you to LeVar Burton for choosing "Control Negro" to read live as part of PRI's *Selected Shorts*. Hearing you read my words was tremendous!

Many thanks to the literary journals and magazines who've published work from this collection: everyone at *Guernica,* including Meakin Armstrong, Autumn Watts, Hillary

Brenhouse, and Morgan Babst, who rescued "Control Negro" from the slush; and the folks at *Phoebe* and at *Prime Number Magazine,* including Taylor Brown, who chose "The King of Xandria" as a winner.

Thank you to the members of my longtime writing group, Kristen-Paige Madonia, Hope Mills Voelkel, Aaron Weiner, Raennah Lorne, and George Kamide. Thanks to UVA's Young Writers Workshop, Writer-House, the Virginia Festival of the Book, New Dominion Bookshop, and our local salon of women writers, begun by Sharon Harrigan. With gratitude to folks who share local Black stories, like Charlene Green, John Edwin Mason, and Lisa Woolfork. Thank you to institutions like the Jefferson School that highlight local Black history, and to the Thomas Jefferson Foundation, for its preservation and care of Thomas Jefferson's plantation home, where I have felt both awestruck and heartsick.

With gratitude to the workshops and residences I've had the privilege to attend with their fabulous teachers and writers: Creative Nonfiction with Lauren F. Winner; FAWC in P-town, led by David Updike; Tin House Summer Workshops, led by Aimee Bender, and again, ten years later, led by Claire Vaye Watkins (where Lance Cleland belted out "Wonderwall"); the ladies at Nimrod Writers, led by Cathryn Hankla and Charlotte Leslie Gregg; the gang at Doe Branch Ink, led by Marjorie Hudson; Southampton Writers Conference, led by Lauren Groff; and the folks at VCCA. Thank you to everyone at Hedgebrook for feeding and caring for women writers like me and for the lush grounds and lovely cabins where we could flip through journal entries of those who came before us. Thank you to my Hedgebrook sisters, Dana Fitz Gale, Elaine Kim, Ashley Lucas, Jaclyn Chan, Mahreen Sohail, Rena Priest, Zeeva Bukai, Margarita Ramirez Loya, Sonora Jha, and Sadia Hassan, with whom I fed fresh apricots to the llamas.

Thank you so much to those who volunteered to read and give feedback or offer big support for these particular stories outside of any workshop and for no good reason. Family and community members, friends and bygone schoolmates, too many folks to name, still I will try: Adam Nemett, Amy Wissekerke, Beth Rader, Bradfield Davison, Conover Hunt, David A. Martin, Dolly Joseph, Eboni Bugg, Elizabeth Bales Frank, Ézé Amos, Jeanne Bollendorf, Jenn McDaniel Russo, Jessica Freemont, Jessica Kingsley, Jim Respess, Joanne Mann, Jody

Hobbs Hesler, Julian Calvet, Lauren Ryan, Leslie M. Scott-Jones, Linda "Mimi" Hunt-Byrd, Marnie Allen, Mary Micaela Murray, Paul Rosen, Phil Varner, Rebecca Duncan, Sebastian Romero, Talia Kolluri, Taylor Harris, Victoria Dougherty, Vijay Owens, and all of you who chimed in on a stray writerly query on social media.

Thank you to those who've taught or read stories or essays that I've written. Thank you to all the writers whose words helped me to more clearly see the world or a place for myself in it.

Thank you to all of my young art students — you are an endless source of inspiration. I hope you keep learning and shaping the world through art forever. Thank you to my dear friends, and to my extended families, aunties and uncles and myriad cousins. Thank you to my storyteller mother, my judicious father, my bighearted big brother, my kind sis-in-law, and my truth-teller son. (I want to leave you a better world, but I'm afraid I may only leave you stories of longing for it.)

Thank you to my partner in life and art-making, Billy, for your encouragement, dedication, and for making me laugh to the point of tears nearly daily. Thank you for talking me off the ledge, and taking all of the photographs, and fixing the tech; for bringing me luxe ramen or the perfect sandwich, and so on: All of it is remembered. All of it is our life. You are a shining star.

ABOUT THE AUTHOR

Jocelyn Nicole Johnson's writing has appeared in *Guernica,* the *Guardian, Phoebe, Prime Number,* and elsewhere. Her short story "Control Negro" was featured in *Best American Short Stories 2018,* guest edited by Roxane Gay, and was read live by LeVar Burton as part of PRI's *Selected Shorts* series. She has received fellowships from Hedgebrook, Tin House, and VCCA. A veteran public-school art teacher, Johnson lives and writes in Charlottesville, Virginia.

The employees of Thorndike Press hope you have enjoyed this Large Print book. All our Thorndike, Wheeler, and Kennebec Large Print titles are designed for easy reading, and all our books are made to last. Other Thorndike Press Large Print books are available at your library, through selected bookstores, or directly from us.

For information about titles, please call:
  (800) 223-1244

or visit our website at:
  gale.com/thorndike

To share your comments, please write:
  Publisher
  Thorndike Press
  10 Water St., Suite 310
  Waterville, ME 04901